PRAISE FOR *BARE A STORI*

"A pitch-perfect, masterfully wrought collection of fiction short in length but vast in the Big Bang of the human condition. *Bare Ana and Other Stories* is a work that will enchant in the reading and will endure in the reader for long, long after."

—Robert Olen Butler, winner of the Pulitzer Prize for Fiction, author of *A Good Scent from a Strange Mountain* and *Late City*

"Robert Shapard co-edited *Sudden Fiction*, an anthology that predated the term flash fiction, and had a ground-breaking effect on the current lay of American short fiction. It's welcome now to have *Bare Ana and Other Stories*, a compelling collection of his own work. These artfully concise stories are stamped with a sense of American place, and set at intersections where the workaday world collides with illumination. There's an ache of the sensual from subtle detail seen freshly enough to elevate the prose, as it does in 'Cardinals,' a story about a couple in a long marriage, in which a line reads 'there were still bra strap indentations in her skin that stirred him.' Were Shapard a pianist, he'd be a musician praised for the beauty of his delicate touch."

—Stuart Dybek, author of *Ecstatic Cahoots* and *Paper Lantern*, winner of a MacArthur Fellowship and the PEN/Malamud Award

"I love how these stories seem to configure doors and windows that open onto scenes we recognize from some deep part of our souls and then go places we would never have imagined."

—Christopher Merrill, author of *On the Road to Lviv*, director of University of Iowa International Writing Program

"I loved every story. A remarkable collection."

—Meg Pokrass, author of *The First Law of Holes: New and Selected Stories*

"An impressive collection, like an introduction to flash fictions."

—Elizabeth Harris, winner of the John Simmons Short Fiction Award and the Gival Press Novel Award, author of *Three Lives of a Woman*

"In Shapard's world, it's always dusk, the light is changing, there's the before and after of a car crash or dust settling, of illicit love and bourbon tossed back. There's a simmering repression here that's not quite rage but is deeply connected to lust and love lost. I glided through these lives, these short bits of lightning, that pulled me gracefully through time, as I hung, glittering like chalk dust in sunlight until the very last word. *Bare Ana and Other Stories* offers readers a collection of carefully crafted and powerful stories."

—Sherrie Flick, author of *Thank Your Lucky Stars*

"Robert Shapard's luminous collection portrays characters lost in the landscapes of nature and of their own making, and characters confronting that transformative juncture where an accident or event changes all. His ability to find and capture transcendency in the smallest of moments—the click of a camera, a ray of sunlight pooling on the floor—will leave his readers enraptured, enlightened, and with a better knowledge of very short fiction."

—Tara Lynn Masih, editor of *The Rose Metal Press Field Guide to Writing Flash Fiction*, founding editor of *The Best Small Fictions*

"Gorgeously written, endearingly weird, hauntingly cool! I like everything about it."

—Tom Hazuka, author of *If You Turn to Look Back*, co-editor of *Flash Fiction Youth*

"The master editor of the flash form offers his own short takes (and a few longer ones) on the world we live in."

—Steve Heller, author of *What We Choose to Remember*, former director of Antioch-L.A. MFA Program

"There's a *Black Mirror* feel to many of these pieces, which I love. Whether 'realistic' or surreal they each stand alone, full of insight and lovely turns of phrase."

—Nancy Stohlman, author of *After the Rapture* and *Going Short: An Invitation to Flash Fiction*

"One of my favorite stories, 'Motel,' would make a great short movie."

—Pamela Painter, author of *Fabrications: New and Selected Stories* and bestselling *What If?*

"'She unbuttoned the fish,' begins one story in Robert Shapard's *Bare Ana*—an arresting statement that turns out to be literal, accurate, miraculous, and perfect. Shapard's fiction works like that. In a volume of very short stories (some flash or sudden fictions, some approaching the short end of the traditional short fiction range), he displays a tour-de-force capacity for invention and a maestro's control. Fiction is as much about what is not said as about what is. Shapard's ear is pitch perfect for voice, and perhaps even more for shocking silences."

—T.R. Hummer, author of *After the Afterlife*, former editor of *The Georgia Review*

"Who could resist these characters, who embrace you with their eagerness to solve the mysteries of unrelenting life."

—James Thomas, author of *Pictures, Moving*, co-editor of *Flash Fiction America*

BARE ANA AND OTHER STORIES

Robert Shapard

Regal House Publishing

Published by
Regal House Publishing, LLC
Raleigh, NC 27605
All rights reserved

ISBN -13 (paperback): 9781646035328
ISBN -13 (epub): 9781646035335
Library of Congress Control Number: 2024935111

All efforts were made to determine the copyright holders and obtain their permissions in any circumstance where copyrighted material was used. The publisher apologizes if any errors were made during this process, or if any omissions occurred. If noted, please contact the publisher and all efforts will be made to incorporate permissions in future editions.

Cover images and design by © C. B. Royal
author photo by Adam Moroz

Regal House Publishing, LLC
https://regalhousepublishing.com

The following is a work of fiction created by the author. All names, individuals, characters, places, items, brands, events, etc. were either the product of the author or were used fictitiously. Any name, place, event, person, brand, or item, current or past, is entirely coincidental.

Regal House Publishing supports rights of free expression and the value of copyright. The purpose of copyright is to encourage the creation of artistic works that enrich and define culture.

Printed in the United States of America

To those who
didn't want to be thanked
I thank you anyway

CONTENTS

Thomas and Charlie

The highway had turned tropical and potholed, two narrow lanes and narrower bridges, with butterflies spattering the grill screen we bought on good advice at the border.

My mother said, "We're on the wrong road." The map was flapping and her hair, still blond then, was flaying, air thudding through the open windows of the Buick. "We're lost."

My father sang "On the Road to Mandalay." Years later my mother said he was sometimes a stranger, after the war, although he never seemed strange to me. He had been in combat both in Europe and the Pacific, but he rarely spoke of it. He worked for an oil company, and we moved often. I was only ten at the time of our vacation, and he died when I was sixteen.

The small patch of tropics, which was not shown on my mother's map but through which we had been traveling, soon thinned out as we climbed into the desert mountains. We followed a big, backfiring diesel that we couldn't pass, and drowsing in the back of the car, in the heat and swaying, I could tell from the backfires when the diesel was leaving us farther behind downhill, or uphill was coming closer again. My father spoke enthusiastically about the great city we were going to, Mexico City, high above everything, ancient and beautiful. Nothing ever changed there. My mother, so practical, consulted guidebooks by the dozen and wrote itineraries. I remember mostly rain and traffic jams.

It was hot and growing dusky when a village appeared below us. Later we found it on the map: Tamazunchale, which my mother pronounced "Thomas and Charlie," a few whitewashed houses in a dusty bend, treetops shimmering in the last of the sun. Ahead of us the diesel was plummeting toward a one-lane bridge, and around the curve on the other side of the village a small green pickup suddenly appeared, flashing its headlights. But the diesel barreled onto the bridge at top speed, not trying to slow at all, so that the pickup, in order to avoid disaster, was forced into a skid on the village side. It flipped and rolled, and as the diesel shot past, the pickup slammed finally onto its side in a wave of dust and gravel.

"God, oh god." We followed slowly downhill in the Buick. When we crossed the bridge, the dust swallowed us, then as it cleared on the other side we saw the underside of the pickup. Some villagers had already reached it. Others were still running, village women with their skirts clutched up, crying. There was a strong smell of Pemex gasoline and around one of the tires was a pale flame. One of the men, wearing white campesino pants but bare chested, stretched down into the skyward window, while others held his ankles, and fetched up a howling infant.

"We've got to stop," my mother said.

Probably there was a farm family in the pickup, which had pink and green tassels and curtains painted on the inside of the windshield, a decoration common to many Mexican trucks. We had slowed almost to a stop, but not entirely. We were going on.

"They need help," my mother said.

"They've got help," my father said.

"We could take them to a hospital," my mother said.

"They'll call for help," my father said.

I watched through the rear window, the villagers crowding around. There were streaks of black in the dust cloud, but never an explosion. The cloud billowed, huge and serene.

"But what if there's no telephone?" my mother said. "How will they call for help?"

The diesel had continued up the mountain. It had not stopped to render aid. It was nowhere in sight.

"You don't know what could happen," my father said. "You don't understand, do you?"

My mother was not a hysterical woman. If there were shouts and tears I don't remember them. If she had doubts, as she always did, about everything in her life, she took refuge in my father's direction.

"They'll think it's our fault," she said reasonably. "They'll come after us. They'll throw us in jail."

My father began to sing "On the Road to Mandalay."

My mother's map flapped furiously. Later she gave him some water from the cap of the big thermos she kept at her feet. When we traveled nights, there were always the embers of the cigarettes they passed between them.

I watched all the way to the top of the mountain. In the evening light, rising above the village, the dust was like a pink bomb blast: a great, unfolding flower. I understood only that my mother and father were lost.

DEEP GREEN LAKE

She unbuttoned the fish—they were in her raincoat pockets—ran the bathwater and released them into the tub. She lit a cigarette and took one of the red pills that Jack called "bombers." It was her birthday, a bright panel of morning sunlight across the tiles, the wall heater ticking in the other room. She wished she was swimming, she wanted applause, for leaping off the deck into the lake, a dark green cold that deafened her, pressing against her ears, seizing her body then yielding. It hurt like hell, the splinter she got on the dock. They cheered at her distress, how she flailed in the water back to the ladder as fast as she could. Then hobbling and collapsing onto her bottom, rolling back like a bug trying to find the splinter in her foot, they laughed at that too. Later, dressed, warm, Band-Aided, she remembered the cheering most. That was last summer. This morning she was more awake than she'd ever been, since four in the morning, getting organized. Now she couldn't remember what for. She hadn't seen Jack in forever. Days. She texted Where r u and he texted back, Take a bomber. So many ideas, scrambling one over the other. Maybe she would never see him again. When the sun came up she took a walk in the park, the air biting, but the raincoat kept her warm almost, it wasn't bad, waiting for the pet store to open. Why fish? She couldn't remember, but at home it was the right idea again. She wanted fish in a lake on a sunny morning in the bathtub where she could control them. She took off her clothes, swallowed a handful of bombers, finding applause in her own lovely, warm, deep green lake.

Sundress

She hadn't seen her children or grandchildren for so long she sometimes forgot she had them. Then Child Protective Services found her. They brought one she didn't know about, a four-year-old grandchild (or was she a great-grandchild?), Lucy. The mother had died of a drug overdose, they said. There was some monetary support involved, there was no one else, so she said all right.

Her house was near the town of Mount Hood, Oregon, not far from the interstate and the railroad and the river, with a view of the mountains beyond. She didn't have internet but got it at the coffee shop in town.

In no time they were close, Lucy and Gram, a great pair, and she began to worry that she might die before the girl was along in her schooling and the other arrangements for her life. Of course Gram quit smoking, but that wouldn't be enough. It always came down to this moment.

Lucy was by her side on the back porch glider, a lovely late afternoon. She said, Sweetie go play in the yard, Gram has something to do. The backyard was large but gated. She didn't keep livestock anymore, just chickens, fruit trees, vegetable and flower gardens.

She went into the house and in the bedroom took off her clothes. In a large closet was the cedar chest she hadn't opened in years. Inside it she found a sundress from long ago. It was so pretty. She laid it out on the bed. In the bathroom she went into a brief trance. Then with a deep breath she pulled off her old skin and dropped it on the hamper. She took a shower and by the time she got out she had changed into a young woman. Her new skin was lustrous and soft and her hair was dark. In the bedroom again she put on the sundress, which she filled beautifully, and went outside to call Lucy.

The girl was near the porch. When she turned, her eyes went wide and she said, Who are you? The young woman said, I'm Gram, can't you see? She said softly, Look close. But the girl's face was set. No you're not. Who are you, where's Gram?

It was all coming back, how terrified a child could be, how bewildered. This time she hoped it would be different. She had to admit she was surprised at her own voice, how young and pleasant it was. Sweetie, she said, It *is* me. I wanted to show you, you can do this too when you get old. No one has to die if they don't want to, isn't that wonderful? She reached to scoop the girl up but she darted away in the gathering evening. I want Gram, she screamed, again and again. It wouldn't be easy to catch her. And what was the point? If a child didn't accept, it was over.

So Gram went back into the house and in the bathroom pulled on her old skin again. In the closet she laid the sundress away and put on her old clothes. Of course the girl didn't want to be alone. How cold to be among strangers. It was the way of the world, not to want to live alone even forever if you could have love instead. She went out the screen door and saw the girl sitting in the dark of the yard. Lucy, she called, clearing her throat.

The girl sat up staring, then ran to her, gulping for a breath, A woman came…she said she was *you!* Oh, she did, did she? Gram said. Well, we won't worry about that, I'm here now. Lucy held her leg fiercely. Gram, she said. *You're* my gram.

It was time to feed the child and put her to bed. In the kitchen afterward she did the dishes, found the cigarettes where she'd hidden them, and poured some whiskey into a jelly glass. Tomorrow she would call Child Protective Services to make other arrangements for the girl. It was best for her. As for herself she could get along without the money, she had before. She had no business raising a child at her age. What if she died?

GLYPH

He'd loved hieroglyphs ever since Indiana Jones twisted one, a stone temple figure, and the walls rumbled open. Now he was just a guy with a sputtering Ducati motorcycle, taking business classes, who fell in love with a girl and took a poetry class to be with her. He learned that all glyphs, hiero or otherwise, were images, which could take form in any of the senses, so her scent in bed was a glyph, her touch was sometimes a glyph, and between her lips, when she said goodbye, though he pleaded for her not to, his name was a glyph.

MOTEL

That night a pickup without its lights on cut across the dirt divider onto the highway in front of us. I had no chance to brake and swerved off the shoulder at sixty miles an hour, snapping down through the brush with no seat belts and Gayle Ann sliding hard against me. We bounced onto and off an access road, missed a pole, and smashed into the back of a motel.

We were in my son's car, his first, a 1952 Buick he was restoring. He was visiting his grandmother. The motel was cinderblock and the Buick went right through it, with a tremendous crump, then an avalanche of thuds and clunks that seemed to go on forever. Finally there was just dust and quiet.

I couldn't breathe. I couldn't move, but inside I was fighting like a diver for air. In the dark the glowing red bips in the instrument panel seemed magical, floating. The windshield was smashed, a dark net full of glitters. Then my breath started coming in squeaks. Gayle Ann was crying. "Charlie, please," she said. She was afraid I was dying.

I was fine. I just couldn't breathe. I was never happier in my life because all that mattered to me was that Gayle Ann was alive. My ribs were bruised, Gayle Ann's elbow was bruised, we had cuts, jammed fingers, bumps, but none of that bothered us. We were indestructible.

I pushed back against the door and got it open enough to squeeze out with Gayle Ann behind me. Up by the highway and beyond the motel there was nothing but scrub brush and moonlight, an August night, late but still hot. We were trembling, shaken but exalted because we were in love and alive, not touching because we were afraid of hurting each other.

The back of the motel was a dark wall, a black pit with a Buick buried in it. I got close and called, "Is anybody in there?" If anybody was in there, some man or a woman or a baby, they could be dead. There was nothing but black silence.

"What about the bourbon?" Gayle Ann said.

We had a bottle from the party in Austin. I had a feeling we were going to get nailed for this. The guy in the pickup was probably drunk. That was the irony. This late at night he could weave all over the highway all the way back to his ranch and sleep it off and never get caught. He would never even remember it.

I went around to the front of the motel. The big sign was off, just the one floodlight shining in front of an empty gravel lot. A neon vacancy sign was glowing pink in the office window.

Along the line of rooms on this side it was dark, but just then a light came on in one of them, so I knocked and a guy opened the door. Dust boiled out of the doorway around us. He was gray and baggy-eyed but not old, some of the gray was dust. He had a big sagging belly and only his undershorts on.

"Is anyone hurt?" I said.

He wanted to say something but had a coughing fit with dust shaking out of his head. I went in. The room was a mess. The front of the car was in it with the hood sprung and flattened with blocks and rubble. The dresser was splintered against the end of the bed. The head of the bed was snapped in two. There was a piece of cinderblock on one of the pillows. It was just lying there like a small pink head. No arms, no legs. Nobody else in the room.

I got down by the wheel well. The light from the table lamp shone under the car in dusty shafts and outside through the gaps. I was coughing too. I shouted, "Gayle Ann!"

Her foot and ankle appeared, standing outside in the dust by a piece of chrome and turquoise metal, which was the lower part of the car door. "What?" She sounded frightened. I thought objectively for the first time what a terrible thing if she had been killed. She had two children. If I were dead it would be terrible, too, but my son was sixteen and could almost take care of himself.

I told her to try and start the car.

"Charlie?" Her voice came closer, her hand planting itself on the ground in a puff of dust. Then her face came down, peering in at me, one eye covered by a fall of hair. "Should we do this?" she said. "What if the engine catches on fire?"

I said, "Just do it."

So she did. The engine turned over with a terrible banging, like somebody trying to axe his way out of a tin washtub. I told her to stop.

The grayish man was sitting on the bed. "I was asleep," he said. His voice was hoarse but at least he could talk now. We introduced ourselves—his name was Russ—and I asked him where we were.

"Texas," he said.

I said, "I know that. I mean what's the next town?"

"Cotulla," he said.

I said I had told Peg, my wife, the day before that I was going to Amarillo. Not that she cared.

"Amarillo," Russ said. "That's about four hundred miles north of here."

I knew that, I said. I asked him if there was a telephone, and Russ said he was sure there was one in the room. We found a television not too badly smashed behind the dresser but no telephone. We heard radio static somewhere outside, and voices. There was a loud knocking and we turned. It was Gayle Ann, horrified, in the doorway of the motel room. "My god," she said.

As far as I was concerned, nothing could ever be wrong with the world as long as Gayle Ann was smiling. The world wasn't right at the moment but at least there was a kind of relief in the way she was agog.

She had the bourbon and I sent her down to the Coke and ice machines that Russ said were by the office, then I helped Russ find his clothes. He was a local rancher. He didn't have a suitcase.

There were empty beer cans by the bed. Butts in an ashtray, with lipstick on them. So there had been a woman in the room. He said at nine o'clock every night the owner switched off the motel lights and passed out. If you were a friend and needed a room, you just went behind the desk and got a key.

I said, "Russ, a pickup cut across the highway, right out of the dark, in front of us."

He found some plastic cups in the bathroom and dislodged a dinette chair from the wall by the bed. The voices were from the car radio, on the other side of the wall—Gayle Ann hadn't switched the ignition key back all the way. Russ said nobody could blame us for having a drink after coming so close to death. That was true. Also, if the highway patrol showed up and wanted to give us a balloon test, it would only prove we had drinks after the wreck, not before. When Gayle Ann got back we made drinks. We were all amazed at being alive.

Russ said he was dreaming when the car smashed into the room. He was in an ancient Mexican temple and could smell the stone. For some reason his cap was on the altar: he knew about human sacrifice and was worried, but there wasn't anybody there.

I said, "Is this a cord? There's something under here that looks like a telephone cord."

Gayle Ann said, "Who are you going to call?"

"There's nothing in Cotulla," Russ said. "The gas pump doesn't open until seven in the morning."

Gayle Ann was flagging. She was in her jeans and sat on the bed cross-legged. I said we could use some lime for the bourbon and Coke. She said we were going to need more than that. We were both beginning to hurt some.

"I'll hire a wrecker," I said. Gayle Ann's husband wasn't due back until Monday. That wasn't what worried me. "We'll tow the car home."

"Two hundred miles?" She looked doubtful.

"My insurance will pay for it." What worried me was that my son wasn't going to understand. I had taught him how to drive, coached his softball team, kissed him good night and tucked him in when he was little, and took him camping. So what? He was going to hate this. It was his first car. It was a wonderful hulk of a car, which is why I took it to the party in Austin, and then on this fucked-up road trip—Gayle Ann loved the car.

"We sleep in, then get all this taken care of by lunchtime," I said. "Then we rent another car, and by tomorrow afternoon we'll be in Laredo strolling around the zocalo under the alamos. Just like we planned. Dinner and drinks at the Cadillac Bar." I sat on the bed and leaned back on my elbow next to Gayle Ann.

"We're only half an hour from the border," I said. "We've got plenty of time."

Gayle Ann had courage. She went over my scalp, checking

for cuts. "You're just like a big old hound dog," she said. Then she said, "Charlie, I love you so much." Russ grinned and ducked his head and looked away. She had never had an affair before.

I said, "Don't worry, we'll get through this."

But we didn't get through it. In the morning the boy would only tow the car as far as his own garage. There weren't any rental cars. The motel owner was an older woman who trembled writing out both of our home addresses and the names of both our insurance agents. Later, drinking coffee and something stronger, she asked if we were staying another day.

But that night, the important thing was Russ and I got the window air conditioner blowing again, and with the door open, that cleared a lot of the dust. I thought we should stay by the car. I told Russ, "Look, do you want to get another room?"

He said sure.

He got a key from the office and came back to say good night, but first he had another drink with us. Outside, Gayle Ann shook out the blanket and sheets. It was so pleasant, late, with a breeze, the lamplight and music still on the car radio. I didn't think Russ was going to leave.

When he did we locked the door, and because we didn't want anybody on the highway seeing the outline of a car buried in a wall, we clicked our light off.

Our eyes grew accustomed to the dark and we fixed another drink. We took awhile getting our clothes off. The moon shone through the window on the grille. It was caved in like a shark's mouth.

We were feverish. Cool air was blowing but our skins were hot and damp and smooth. The moonlight made our bare feet glow.

Big Bug Love

I'm sitting in the windowsill when—*poom!*—my mate hits the screen. He whirs his wings, fumbles around the screen until he finds a way under and comes high stepping his way to me—oh, he is one good-looking bug who won't be denied.

It's the same for the girl I share this apartment with when her man comes knocking. She says, Where have you been all week? He says, I love you, and she says, Ha. It doesn't matter if she's hungry and tired, just home from work, *he* wants to get a buzz on. I can't live this way, she says. But she lets him drag her into the bedroom.

I can't deny my mate and I are humming. Our feelers are all over each other. He's going *nung, nung, nung, nung, nung,* crazy as always, and there's always that shock in my joints that makes me buck and grab. Before I know it, I've torn his head off, and I'm eating it. It's like a terrible dream. But it's a lovely one, my heart *thrumming, thrumming.* Unfortunately, I wake up and see my lover has fallen to pieces, and it doesn't help that this has happened before.

Last week, for her, it was different. There was a fight: She cried and kicked him out, and he hasn't been back. Since then I've sat motionless every night in the window, thinking, I can't live like this—but what other way is there?

I try to imagine what if she lived like me.

First of all, she'd have a dead body on her hands. Then what would she do? Nothing for a while—just sleep, all day if she had to. She'd store up energy then wake before evening and wrap him in the sheet. Push him off the bed and pull him sliding over the bedroom floor, across the kitchen linoleum, out the back door. She'd wedge him under the porch railing until he slipped through. It's a second-floor apartment, so he'd fall a long way and hit the mud with a *whack*. Then she'd try to forget him. It's not easy losing a lover. Sometimes it takes courage just to make it from one hour to the next. To be on the safe side, she'd stay motionless. What if someone heard the *whack* and saw a sheet below their window, the blunt form of a thorax underneath, and a leg that's come out? She has to be ready to fly away.

But probably nothing would happen—the woods are dark and close in back, and the sound would be muffled by street traffic on the other side of the apartments. In a little while, she'd go in to clean up. Sponge the kitchen, working back toward the bedroom where most of the blood would be. Stuff his clothes in a black garbage bag. Mop and rinse and throw clean sheets on the bed. Then she could take her shower and wash him out of her hair, singing, *Empty, empty, empty, empty.* I do that sometimes. On a hot evening like this, she could go out on the front porch where it's cooler to comb out her wet tangles. The first star would have appeared. The air would be perfumed with the scent of charcoal-grilled meat, like tonight, with voices not far away—people laughing, having drinks in the parking lot.

I know this: she may kick him out, but she doesn't want to hurt him.

It's just that she has to protect herself. And now she has to forget. She needs to move on, probably to another apartment, in another part of town. There's nothing to do now. It's getting dark, and the mercury vapor lamps are filling the parking lot with their greenish-silver light. She turns to go in and sees a young man standing under the balustrade looking up at her. He says, Hello, it's hot tonight, isn't it? He asks if she'd like a cold beer—he's got one in his hand and holds it up and waggles it.

Thanks, I don't think so, she says, I've had a hard day. She feels exposed—her terry robe is much too small.

He's already coming up. He stops on the stair below her and offers her the beer. It's okay, I won't bother you, and he smiles.

She seems relieved and relaxes a little. Why is he drawn to her?

I know: her legs in this light are silvery like mine. She can't deny he's beautiful—she's seen him around, confident and very nice the way he's high stepped up to her. She swings her hair back, says, All right, I wouldn't mind, and holds out her hand. What other way is there to live?

APERÇUS

At the turn of the twentieth century a movement in self-improvement swept Europe. Its leader, a French psychologist named Émile Coué, wrote, "If you want to change your life, you must capture aperçus."

Amanda discovered him in the French language course she was taking.

For Coué, aperçus were instants of cosmic awareness, conjured by almost anything, whether a bit of memory, a few musical notes, even a scent. Everyone has them, but few remember or even recognize them because they pass so quickly. To capture an aperçu, Coué said, one had only to say the words, *This is the meaning of my life.*

"Practice this daily," he instructed. "If you are diligent, you will begin to see your place in the universe. If you are suffering, you will begin to heal."

Amanda was skeptical. How could just repeating a phrase, *This is the meaning of my life*, really change anything? Some people couldn't change if you paid them. She wasn't sure she needed healing. Still, she was interested to try.

Her boyfriend, Andy, moved her iPad aside in bed and said, "If anything can prompt an aperçu, then can one aperçu prompt another aperçu? And then another, like a chain reaction? Like a mental orgasm? Would that be dangerous? It can't be good." She put her hand like a claw gently over his mouth. "Is that what you think of me?" she said.

He kissed the top of her leg, the crease, down to her pubic hair. "Marry me," he said.

"Just shut up," she said.

They'd only known each other a month. He'd asked her out right away, when they met at Austin Plumbing Supply, where she worked. He was looking for designer faucets. It turned out they went to the same college, and had a mutual friend who was a performing musician. They were playing a gig together that night and he said if she came he would take care of her. Which she did, with her work friend Dolores. She loved it when he sang harmony, and his mandolin solo on "I'll Fly Away." She couldn't get him or the song out of her mind.

After that they were with each other every night. When he asked her, again, to marry him, she said sure, but there were just two problems. He was still in the process of getting a divorce, and she was getting over a boy she met two years ago who did too many drugs, never grew up. It wasn't easy getting free of him, getting clean herself. She'd gone back to college part-time as part of her recovery, taking small contract jobs like the one for Austin Plumbing, upgrading their old inventory system. Now she was four courses short of getting her accounting degree, taking French to complete her language requirement— because what was the point of taking Spanish if everyone in her family already spoke Tex-Mex?

As for the famous Émile Coué, what she wanted from him and his aperçus was perspective. A calm way to think separate from accounting numbers. She wasn't sure if it would work. If she took a sip of a margarita and remembered drinking too many at a party once and retching violently, was that an aperçu? Or if she saw an old Buick that reminded her of her dead grandmother's car, was that supposed to be *the meaning of her life?*

They often drove to Dallas to stay with her brother, who had a house near Love Field, the commuter airport, where the properties were cheap. Her brother, who loved her, who'd taught her to drive when she was twelve in a crappy old convertible he'd bought at a used car lot. They went everywhere. They'd even crossed a bridge to downtown after a spring flood, the river still vast and thundering just under their wheels. She was scared, but somehow it was all right because he was her older brother and would protect her. Their father had left them. She'd already begun to travel with her mother from apartment to apartment, from one school to another. After a few years her mother was gone too. Now her brother was home, all she had left.

She'd asked Dolores, "What kind of guy asks somebody to marry him if he still has a wife?" Dolores was her mother's age. "You'd be surprised," she said. Amanda said, "I'm only twenty-seven." Dolores raised her eyebrows, nodded, and said, "You can't wait forever." They agreed the question was whether to trust his divorce was actually happening. Dolores looked him over when he came into Austin Plumbing again. "He needs a haircut," she reported. His hair was sandy, spilling from the sides and back of his ball cap.

Andy was renovating an old frame house he owned. He let her know the divorce papers were signed. And more. His ex-wife and daughter lived in Houston, he'd grown up on a ranch, had been in the army in Iraq, then Italy, and had worked construction. The house was surrounded by beautiful old shade trees, was a mess but livable. He owned an apartment house, too, and sometimes took things in trade for rent—he said it probably made him an idiot. His treasure was an authentic African harp, with a cracked gourd. He sat in with bands around Austin, playing not just mandolin but anything that had an *o* on the end—banjo, Dobro, mando. She said, "What about *oboe*?" She was tutoring him in French. When he tried to say, "I like your face more than any other in the world," she looked away and said, "Your accent is getting better." In a side yard there were refrigerators, tilting like Easter Island heads. In the turn-around, a bass boat full of leaves.

"You've got everything," she said. "Why would you need me?"

He gazed at her and said in English, "You would be nice to have around."

She liked his answer. She didn't mind the clutter. But she thought, *Am I a trade-in?* And, *Is this the meaning of my life?*

Her most lasting aperçu vision came while they were at a party at her brother's house. Friends and in-laws and neighbors were in the kitchen and backyard, but she'd gone upstairs to lie down, after the long drive from Austin. It had been a rainy day and the air was damp but pleasant by the open window. Laughter and voices floated up, and from somewhere came the music from a bygone time, the Big Band era, when her great-grandmother was young. The melody and orchestration were haunting and she had an aperçu, a distinct feeling that she was born already knowing "April in Paris" and "Sentimental Journey." The vision grew, a beautiful, living lacework of natural patterns—the return of spring rains, the music returning, coming home to her brother again, bringing a boyfriend home again. She'd brought boyfriends home before, but none of them had been good for her. Did she only come home when things were already failing? *Is this the meaning of my life?* she wondered. In the same moment, she realized that whatever the meaning of her life was, she had to choose. An aperçu couldn't tell her what to do.

Sleepy, she thought of other visions she'd had, like being on the bridge with her brother, the flood just under her feet. Without thinking, she stepped out onto the water and walked on it—how easy it was. She looked back for her brother but instead saw Andy, out on the water, arms flailing, because the water was slippery. He looked vulnerable, wearing nothing but his shorts and ball cap. She realized he was trying to rescue her. She yelled above the roar, "You really do love me, don't you?" His cap flew off and he fell scrambling onto his hands and knees. He didn't answer, but kept coming. "It's dangerous out here," she yelled, "but don't worry, I've chosen an aperçu!" He looked relieved, and lost. She wanted to laugh, he was so sweet and funny, and she stretched her hand toward him so they could be swept away together.

TURTLE CREEK

At midnight the rain had stopped. We all heard the bang of impact. Then the police were at the door. Some people panicked and ditched their drug of preference, oxy, molly, special K. On the front porch somebody said they heard a scream before the impact, someone said it was a girl on a scooter, and another said a guy was holding on behind her. We walked downhill to the bridge, which spanned the creek at the end of the block. The wreck scene was strobing like red and blue disco lights. Fire truck, EMS, police cars. A halo of plastic and metal bits glittering where the scooter hit the bridge. The crushed remains of the scooter were there but no girl or guy. Probably they'd flown over the rail into the creek and been swept away. We never knew who they were. The creek was thundering. It was the end of summer. A lot of us went on to college, which a lot of us didn't finish. Years later, the drowning was all some of us remembered from high school. The thundering creek, the cops, the strobing lights, the drugs, the summer rain starting again, washing us all away.

LOBSTER

Eddie said to send the lobster first class or whatever it took to get it to Wyoming alive and reasonably happy so they could boil it to death there. He made her smile, talking like that.

She'd fallen in with him yesterday afternoon at the fundraiser, on probably the largest private lawn on Cape Cod. He said he was crazy about her, she said why, and he said because you are endearingly geeky. Then he offered her a job with the campaign, though it wasn't clear he had the power to do so.

The party went on into the night and at last they found a room, in the gable of a house, bumping heads on the slanted ceiling, first him on top then they reversed, grappling in the single bed. Afterward, Eddie dropped—more like imploded—into sleep, and she tried the same but it was fitful. She groped her way down a dark hall to a bathroom, feeling fraudulent because she'd pretended to know more than she really did about social media strategy. Really she was just a humble second-year law student. Eddie had been with the presidential campaign since June. He had already passed the bar.

In the morning when she woke because he was bumping around getting dressed, he told her, Don't get up. It'll be so great if you can make it to Wyoming, but it's hugely important to send the lobster. He bent over the covers but she shrank away. You might want to rethink me, she said. No, I will not rethink you, he said. Speaking from beneath the comforter she said, How do I send it? I'm maxed out on my credit card. He wrote instructions on a scrap of paper and was gone.

Two hours later she strode into town with her weekender bag and a headache, trying to feel confident. The fisherman said yes, he had her lobster. She watched him put it in a battered grapefruit box, lined with a garbage bag and wet seaweed— Cape Cod's best, he grinned. She understood this was going to burnish Eddie's reputation for ingenuity in filling odd requests from presidential aides. Possibly it could help earn him a place in Washington after the election. She lugged the box and her bag across the road to a dark bar where men were downing shots and had coffee and a Danish then took the town's only taxi to the airport.

On the way the Cape seemed empty, almost haunted—it was so crowded only a few days ago—now it was September, cool with a front coming in, winds gusting this way and that. She felt disconnected—literally, because her phone battery was dead. If only she could fly to Wyoming like Eddie said. Nancy Rossi, her friend on the law review who invited her to the party, had urged her to come because it was history and exciting—how often did a presidential campaign happen? But Nancy wasn't broke; she had money, it was easy for her.

Coming over the dunes in the taxi it became obvious—she could borrow the money. But not from Nancy, then who?

The airport terminal was a single-wide mobile home with two wooden steps to a passenger lounge with a small electric heater and half a dozen people seated in plastic chairs. A man behind the ticket counter was chatting to someone in his head-set. She waved to get his attention and asked if she could charge her phone. She said she needed to send a lobster.

He said, You want a ticket for Bob?

She said, No, not Bob, a lobster, it has to go on the next flight.

Not unless you want to buy him a seat, he said.

His mic distracted him for a moment, then he said to her with a kind look, There's no cargo space and almost no luggage space left.

She followed his glance at the window—speckled with rain—to the plane outside, parked on an irregular patch of asphalt. It looked tiny—a seven-seater.

I can take him in the co-pilot seat, he said, but I'll have to charge regular passenger fare. He shrugged, as if to say people do this sometimes, then listened to his headset again.

That left so much to decide. In a big hurry. Her parents would never loan her money to fly a lobster somewhere. They would want her to return to school. Auntie Lynne might back her—she was her childhood hero, a lawyer in Vermont who handled prenups, wills, trusts, divorces, all the most important things in people's lives. Now she was more like a friend—usual-ly harried, like last summer, hair straying across her face as she talked a volunteer out of Dunkin' Donuts and to her office to witness a signing, then picked up the kids, and between oth-er clients called Geek Squad to come fix a computer disaster. Meanwhile Uncle Jack was off hiking. He thinks he's Robert Redford, she said, and that's okay.

The man behind the counter announced to the passenger lounge, We'll start boarding in a few minutes. He said, Miss, did you want to buy that ticket?

People stirred. Her cell phone was charged now. Damn, she thought, forcing herself to be calm, looking at the lobster in his box—she couldn't help but think of him as Bob now—weighing options: (1) Send Bob in the co-pilot seat to Boston to connect to Wyoming and his eventual death. (2) Dump Bob, because it went against her grain to buy a seat for a lobster instead of a human being, such as herself. And there were subsets: (2b) It was reasonable to return to law school, but she dreaded it because, as she admitted now, she wasn't the greatest student. (2c) Hurry up and call Auntie Lynne to charge both her and Bob's flight all the way to Wyoming because Eddie *did* want to see her, she *did* want to be with him, she *did* know about social media strategy, anyway more than a lot of people. She would have to make the argument to Auntie Lynne in one sentence—she remembered her saying the law was full of impossible choices.

The man behind the counter stood and pulled on his jacket and pilot cap.

She looked out the window and realized the runway was like one of those long driveways through the dunes to cottages she saw coming up the Cape from Wellfleet almost lost in the coastal grass rolling in the breeze this way and that, and she realized all her choices were right and how beautiful it was, how beautiful it all was.

Two Phenomena of Roughly Equal Importance

"The air on Mars—what there is of it—is leaking away," he said. "About half a pound a second sputtering into space. *P-p-poof.* Stripped away by solar winds." He was still in bed reading a NASA report in the Sunday *New York Times*.

It was a month since she'd moved into his house, more like a cottage, with a tiny yard. They'd dated in college, then hadn't seen each other in ten years, happened to run into each other and remembered they liked each other. They were still learning how to talk to each other again.

"I got so stoned once," she said. "I lay on the floor and listened to the air squeaking in the vents all day. I thought I was on another planet. That was about a year after I met my jerk ex-husband."

He said *mp*, waited a respectful five seconds, and put his iPad on the bedside table. "Mars's early atmosphere used to be like Earth's," he said, "but it didn't have a magnetic field like Earth's to hold it close. Now it's just wisps."

It wasn't working, she thought. Not that she was giving up. In one motion she slipped out of her exercise pants and panties, hopped up on the bed, and did a graceful half roll toward him. "When I think of space, I think of the attic," she said. "I thought I heard something up there last night, did you?"

He liked to kiss the inside of her knee. She couldn't understand why, but was patient about it.

In college they'd had only three dates. On the third, he'd given her his engineering society pin and kissed her passionately. She said, Okay, weirdly pleased. He was not at all bad looking. But by the end of the evening she was freaked out by the whole idea of the pin and gave it back when he took her home. He shook her hand, *shook her hand.* And they went on to other people. She'd liked him, though.

Now, in their early thirties, they were both divorced. She was childless, he had a daughter, who lived with his ex in a nearby city. He drove up or flew up every other weekend. He was an ecological engineer, worked for Boeing for a while, then went out on his own as a consultant. Lately all he could get was low-level number crunching. Yesterday he was out at the lake evaluating a small dam, which he said beavers could have built better. She thought beavers were sweet but weren't that important. Should he be competing with them? Before that he had a job with a Bay Area steel mill, designing scrubbers for their smokestacks, but got laid off because the political winds had changed. That she could understand. Politics had been her life. She had a poly-sci degree, from a good program, was a Democratic party girl (her words), then lost her way, marrying a conservative politician who cheated on her. Ever surrounded by ambition, she'd grown bitter and snarky. After the breakup she had devised her own recovery program by temporarily working for an animal shelter and training for the Ironman. She told friends it took an iron will not to bring home a pet from the animal control shelter. She didn't want to bond with it. Another breakup would be too much pain.

Now, even though they only had three dates in college, they were like old lovers, with new ground rules. They agreed not to talk about love. She let him know how she felt by patting him down before he jogged out to the park, a joke, to make sure he didn't have his engineering pin with him in case he wanted to kiss another woman. In response he said, "It's just chemistry, mine's attracted to yours." He had a tin ear, but she could live with it.

Then why was she feeling so nettlesome this morning? His wife and daughter hadn't lived here for a year, but she felt like any minute they'd come bustling in the door with groceries or after-school friends.

He had quit kissing her knee, and started working his way up the inside of her thigh. "Is that supposed to drive me crazy?" she said, not meaning to sound snarky.

"No, it's to drive me crazy," he said. "Think of me as a spacecraft coming in to dock."

"I see," she said. "Are we going somewhere? In space I mean?" She sighed. "I'm not trying to ruin your day, I just like to make sense of things."

"None of it makes sense without us," he said. "It makes sense if we want it to, you and me."

He eased beside her, head even with hers, pinned her hand comfortably back, his fingers interlaced with hers.

"You sound like some poly-sci theorist," she said.

He fell silent. She'd done it now. Again. Silenced him. His default was to not talk. She squeezed his hand and got no response. It could be over, she thought.

But he said, with effort, "As long as I have you…maybe I can figure out what's important."

It wasn't something her ex had ever said. Or anyone else she could remember. This is a breakthrough, she thought.

She did a dope slap, to keep from crying. "Duh, of course, what's going to prevent those particles from the sun from stripping away Earth's atmosphere too? We have to save our atmosphere. Is there enough oxygen in the spacecraft? We have to dock together." She was babbling.

He said *mp* softly in her ear. "You're a good listener," he said. "Module coming in to dock. Permission to enter," he said.

She realized *mp* was a small laugh. "It's so polite in space. It's nice to ask permission first. Am I the spaceship?" she said. "Are you going to knock first?" He let out a groan, having already entered. He managed to say, "What?"

"Never mind," she said. "I'll just keep talking and..." It seemed right to begin to lose track of what they were saying. "Just keep...keep knocking."

DUMMY

The main thing to do was get out of town but I couldn't help hanging around all summer. One day my mother called and I went to the house.

"Your father's gone out to the room," she said, meaning the quarters used mostly for storage next to the garage. She was pale, blinking. Usually she had her wits about her but now she seemed frightened, rubbing the back of her hand. "I should have called the police," she said. "He won't open the door."

I went through the kitchen trying to stay calm as if I were going to hunt for sandwich makings while she told me about her and Dad's plans for the evening, though they hadn't had evening plans for a long time. She followed me to the key hooks on the back porch.

"Where's the key?" I said.

It had been in her hand the whole time and she gave it to me. "It's the screen that's locked, not the door. I'm sure he's in there. He won't talk to me."

"Call 911," I said, without any force.

I went out through the garden my father had made of the backyard. It was nothing but shadeless dirt when we first moved in. My brother and kids in the neighborhood wrestled while my father dug and planted all day with a flowerpot saucer for an ashtray, sipping from his gin and tonic, sometimes drinking bugs that had drowned in it. As we grew older we helped build the deck and brick walks and the pond gone weedy now. The oaks he planted were now as high as the house. He wasn't the best coach in our sixth-grade football league but was there every game. He taught and acted at the college and we liked it when he came to the dinner table in costume, as the Sheriff of Nottingham, the Gentleman Caller, or King Lear mad and hoary, using his imagination to fall in love with my mother over and over for more than thirty years.

I opened the gate next to the garage and the quarters. I pressed my face against the screen door, which was battered and rusty. The room was L-shaped and dark except for sunlight from the window on the other side. I could see the rolled ends of some rugs.

"Dad?"

There was no sound coming from the room, and outside just the cicadas and birds, someone calling maybe down the alley, a screen door slapping.

"Dad, I know you're in there." He was up to one of his tricks. I was sick of them.

I found a trowel in one of the many flowerpots along the clapboard siding of the quarters and worked it into the crack between the door and the doorjamb, but the metal bent and all I did was gouge the wood and chip the paint. I kicked in the screen, which I should have done in the first place. It was rusty and my foot went right through. I kicked more until I could reach my arm in and flip up the hook.

He was on the floor, half on the rug, half on the linoleum,

next to some cardboard boxes full of junk. His head was under a chair with the stuffing coming out of the armrests; the chair was piled with junk, too, a framed print with the glass cracked. It was hot and the room smelled of tar paper and mildew. A big glass on the floor half full of gin and tonic, no ice, but the glass still sweating, sunlit dust on the chair legs, the stink of cigarette smoke. Dad had on the clothes he wore in the role of Gentleman Gardener: tennis shoes, L. L. Bean khakis, a dress shirt with rolled sleeves. His arms were open at his sides, two dark blue towels from the kitchen wrapped around his wrists and a razor blade on the floor.

"Godammit," I yelled. "Call 911!"

The precinct station was only a few blocks away, down by the branch library. Was my mother calling? There was a burst of birds out of the eaves, and I saw her in the driveway. The window glass was dusty and she seemed far away, waiting in the sun of some long-ago summer, before she took the job at the library, before the college had not renewed my father's contract because of his drinking. Before I was in my second year of high school, got in trouble, and ran away from home. Even so, my father brought me home again and I graduated.

I kneeled by my father. I couldn't see his face under the chair. He had lost weight, in the last year especially. In the evening light the skin of his forearms looked like old paper. There was nothing left of him. His clothes didn't fit. His khakis might as well have been stuffed with the crinkled onionskin pages of the scripts for the radio soap operas he wrote before the war, in New York, where he acted off-Broadway, when Hollywood was a possibility. But we kids were born by then. My mother and father wanted us to grow up in their hometown, where the little theater movement was active.

"Now what?" I asked my father, then to myself, *Now what, now what?*

My father didn't answer. His chest was still, that frail cavity, but he wasn't fooling me.

The screen door opened. It was the police, an older sergeant I'd seen before and a younger patrolman behind him bumping rescue gear against the doorframe. The sergeant looked angry and at the same time a little embarrassed. He had worked this neighborhood for a long time. I tugged my father out from under the chair. I was angry and embarrassed too. We had all done this before.

But this time it was different. It wasn't my father.

It was a dummy.

Old paper in fact, I saw now, stuffed into his old clothes, with a burlap sack for a head. The mouth was crudely drawn in black marker. The half-circles, drawn in black, indicated closed eyes.

I looked at the police. The police looked at me. I was amazed at their faces. They were anguished. The afternoon had come unmoored. Behind them in the door, it was evening. I cradled the dummy against my chest. The burlap face scratched my cheek.

SECOND-RATE WASP

It was a second-rate wasp, one of those buzzing around the wild fig tree, weaving along the porch rail, giddy with autumn. It had a few weeks to live at most, until the temperature dipped below freezing. Another had gotten into a closed travel bag in the house—how did it manage that? I shooed it outside. That was a first-rate wasp, one with a travel plan. But he wouldn't make it to winter, unless he was a female, who could live for several seasons.

My father was inside fixing a drink. He was a chronic alcoholic, more like a second-rate wasp. Lately he'd seemed feverish, trying to get from one drink to another. He'd abandoned dignity. I'd say, Dad, you can get a drink when we get home, or, We'll stop at the liquor store on the way back, okay? I was the only one who could still talk to him. I knew he suffered. I just wanted him to make it to my brother's wedding. I just wanted him to make it to the divorce consultation. I bribed with promises, though I could tell he didn't trust them, or anyone's. Instead he'd lash out. A counselor told me it wasn't personal, it was physiological. It was denial. The trust had been leached out of him.

At least he was still eating. Dad, we've already got plenty of peanuts, I'd say at the grocery store, or, Dad, those are pepperoncini, you said you didn't like them, they're too acidic. Now he wanted them anyway. And figs, we stopped in the produce section and he said, I always loved these. I knew he wouldn't be with us long, but I wanted his last days to be like autumn, like a wasp weaving his way in a beautiful autumn.

BARE ANA

We're in Chinatown, above Honolulu Harbor. We've made a great discovery: an ancient tattoo parlor. Get this, it has 2-D photos on the walls of tats from back in the twenty-first century. We're on a delayed honeymoon, I'm more in love with Ana than ever. She's eight months pregnant, and we're here to get a prenatal tattoo for our unborn baby. The parlor smells wonderful, like the ocean, like clove, with a hint of rotten banana—in other words, gene serum. We call hello and a woman's voice in back calls, "Be there in a minute." Ana peers through the beaded curtain. There's a lab with a recliner and a surgical stool. A pulsing tat string hangs off it, held in place by a coffee mug. Ana looks panicky, and I say, "Are you sure?" She says, "Yes."

I have to tell you about Ana. She's unusual, not because she's so pregnant. You've heard of people who don't have tattoos but you probably never saw one. Ana's completely bare. As for me, I'm normal: I was dark with tattoos by the time I was ten. When we fell in love last year in college, Ana said it was me she loved, not my tats. I had to laugh. I said, "How are my tats not me?" They're me more than anything. I chose them, whereas everything else about me is a pre-nate gene correction, including my straight teeth. I don't say that's wrong. If our parents didn't do that, we'd probably all get diabetes or schizophrenia in our teenage years. Ana never had a father. Her mother was beautiful, covered with tats like vines that were really cursive letters in all the names of her huge family where she was no longer welcome. She was Malayan or Irish or something. She and Ana were close, and she never let Ana get a tat.

The tat woman comes out from the back wearing hospital scrubs. She looks African and has lavender Celtic spirals down to her jaws that bring out the shape of her face. When she sees Ana, her eyes widen.

"We want a pre-nate," I say, half expecting her to warn us it's too late to be safe.

She smiles, palms together in namaste. She says, "What's the child's name?"

Ana flares. "I don't want my baby's name tattooed on her like a label." She turns away quickly, looking at the 2-D photos.

The tat lady blinks at me. She smiles again. "Did you have an image in mind?"

I say no. She goes to the stem in the middle of the room and tries to get it to work. The place is really ancient. She has to bump the stem with her fist—at last, a hologram rushes into the air, trembling. It's just a commercial.

"Drat," she says. "Just give me a minute."

Ana sits on the bench by the window. It's supposed to be a joyous occasion, but she looks like she wants to cry.

I'm not pushing her into this. Last year, she told me what it was like growing up, people staring at her like she was a freak with some kind of skin disease. At the same time, she was used to it and her mother made it a matter of pride. But now her mother was gone, just last year, and she didn't want her own child to go through it. She and I know a pre-nate tat is a priceless gift. It's your identity at birth; it says your parents care. Anyway there's the negative to avoid—we all know what it means to be "born bare."

But call me crazy. I don't care. If Ana's not right with it, I don't want to do this. I say, "Let's go."

She says, "Wait." She says, "I want you to choose a tattoo and don't tell me what it is. I don't want to see it."

I say, "Ana, be serious."

Most parents decide these things together. But she's pleading with her eyes, and I think, Okay, so we're not like most parents. I see the logic. Refusing to choose, she can be true to her mother. Yet, by letting me choose, our daughter can be born normal.

I like it.

I try to think of an image. Of course, there's our daughter's name in kanji, but that's writing and Ana just told the lady she didn't want that. So I start thinking of classics like Maori arm bands, except in class last year, Ana was against usurping native expression. I think of ancient images—panther, heart, rose— and nothing seems right. I begin to despair, but just as I'm glancing at Ana, something strange happens. Her face begins to glow from the sun in the window. Until now, it's been dark and raining all day. What could be more romantic: sunset over the harbor, Chinatown. As the clouds break apart, the sunlight rushes through them like a fiery dragon, flying ahead of the night. This is the image for our daughter's prenatal tattoo. It's been given to us. I know Ana sees it, too, but we won't talk about it.

Instead I whisper it, quietly so Ana won't hear, to the tat lady waiting at the stem. She brings up a series of dragon holos. I pick one—not Disney, not gothic, but Malayan, in honor of Ana's mother. We work on it, darkening lines, adding pearlescence. Then there's positioning: eenie, meenie, miney, mo, ears, buttocks, belly, toe.

Ana lets out a yelp. She's not looking at us but smiling to herself. "Wow, the baby really kicked," she says.

In the lab behind the beaded curtain, we put Ana in the recliner. We inject the gene line and fix it so it's not uncomfortable. There's no problem keeping her from seeing any image, especially on the old equipment this parlor's got. You know the rest—basically, a few keystrokes.

We pay and go out into the evening, laughing, feeling wonderful. It's like the excitement you have as a kid when you get tatted at the mall. Your parents tell you, Calm down. You won't see a thing for weeks. That's how a gene tat works, they say. Nothing but bare skin while it grows deep inside you. Then, because you're a kid, you get bored and almost forget, until one day, on the school bus or in the mirror—*whoom*—there it is, the tat blooming in your skin. Of course, for us the blooming happens to the baby in the womb, not to me or Ana, but the excitement's the same.

The funny thing is, over the next few weeks, I start to worry. Ana says, "Don't worry. Nothing horrible will happen." It's true we don't believe that epigenetic stuff you hear—how methylation can warp an unborn's tat if you wait too late in a pregnancy. It's just with a pre-nate you can't be sure of anything until the birth. I wish we could delay it a week or even two. Instead, the baby is ready to be born a day early.

We rush to the hospital. All night, nothing happens. Then, in the morning, it's moving fast again: Ana sweating, pushing, breathing, the baby's head crowning. I'm holding Ana's hand when the baby is born. I can't see because the nurse is in the way, but I hear the baby's tiny, coughing cry. At last, the doctor holds the baby up.

The dragon seems alive. Its scales are a shimmery green and

silver. Black talons reach around the baby's shoulder and neck, and red fangs frame her forehead. I'm stunned: it's exactly what I wanted.

As he pulls his gloves off, the doctor says in a hearty voice, "Congratulations. That's a fine dragon."

The nurse murmurs, "Yes, it's the best one this week." She's not interested in the tat but in getting the baby into Ana's arms.

Ana doesn't say anything for a moment, looking at the baby. She seems exhausted from her labor, weak and sleepy. Then she whispers, "Oh, she's beautiful."

But I know she's not even seeing the dragon. I start seeing things through Ana's eyes, like I'm on some kind of high. All she sees are the baby's little fingers, which are perfect and bare. The baby's little wrists, mouth, ears, and eyes—all bare, bare, bare.

MAYUMI AND KENZO

For their honeymoon, Mayumi and Kenzo flew to Waikiki, where Kenzo leaned out from the balcony to photograph the sunset, lost his balance, flung the camera to Mayumi as he desperately reached for the rail, and fell twelve floors to his death. "Don't you want me in the picture?" she had said, the moment before, not out of vanity but to distract him from the sunset: Kenzo had always been foolish and risk taking. It was one of the things Mayumi loved about him.

She was stunned, then lightheaded. Out there was the tropical sunset, representing everything romantic and free and yearning. Down there was Kenzo, like a tiny rag doll, with an ink stain spreading from his head on the concrete. Mayumi's hands trembled at the rail. She could not imagine life without Kenzo.

Before they married, Mayumi's *tansu* chest, in the small apartment in Tokyo that she shared with two friends, was so full of the photographs of her and Kenzo's lives together she could hardly close the little drawers. She and Kenzo were of one mind, but it was Kenzo, most of all, who insisted everything had to be photographed. Usually, they were with other university students, the girls almost always posing with their fingers making *V*s, whether they were near Mt. Fuji or under the cherry trees in the park or in the nightclub after graduation when everyone looked so sinister and hilarious in their sunglasses.

There was no horseplay, though, when the two of them posed in front of the Imperial Palace: Kenzo's parents would not approve. Mayumi wondered if she was welcome, the day she and Kenzo visited them. Kenzo's mother was so stiff, so somber, when she and Mayumi posed in front of the garden shed. Mayumi had no choice but to agree with her future mother-in-law's plan to train her in flower arranging, once she had proved herself capable with the more basic chores, such as clipping, tying, and raking. It would be the same with everything else, such as in the kitchen: first, the basic chores, cleaning and chopping, then perhaps she would be allowed to cook.

Kenzo's parents had even added a small bedroom where Mayumi and Kenzo were to live, at least for the first few years of their marriage. Mayumi knew Kenzo was worried she would not be happy there. Because his job was in the center of Tokyo, Kenzo would have to spend hours every morning and evening on the train. His parents' suburb was so far away! There's no sky there, he complained, nothing but fog. Yet most disturbing to Mayumi was that, as the marriage neared, more and more she did not appear in Kenzo's photographs, especially the ones he took near his parents' home. Often there was no one in them at all. Only the rain on every surface, glistening, curving away to the city. For Kenzo, even this had to be photographed, otherwise it was not real, not documented, not validated.

At the railing, Mayumi had no sense of time passing. Nothing seemed real. Then she understood what to do and ran for the elevator, hardly realizing until the descent began that there was a man in the elevator, who asked her what was the matter. At least, that was what she thought: she couldn't have said for sure whether he had spoken in Japanese or English. When they reached the ground floor, she said, "Please, will you do what I tell you?" He followed her as she raced to the side of the hotel and the parking lot where Kenzo had fallen. Although there were cars in the lot, it was away from the street and seemed nearly abandoned. At the far end, a woman was hurrying away. Was she going for help?

Mayumi felt as if she were flying, floating, she was so dizzy and out of breath. She knew she must fight to be rational. Others were there, standing well back from Kenzo's body. Speaking carefully, she said, "That man is my husband. Please call an ambulance." The man from the elevator had caught up to her and was repeatedly moaning the word "holy" or "oh." Turning to him, she handed him the camera. She had been carrying it the whole time, yet it seemed so strange in her hand now: she wanted nothing more to do with cameras. Nonetheless, she forced herself to look. Although the lot was in shadow between buildings, beyond them was a line of ocean and sky. The clouds were disappointingly dull but with a hint of rose, and there was even a palm tree. Without knowing whether she would have the strength, she dropped to the concrete on her knees and cradled Kenzo. She pulled him up, higher. Then she rocked back so that their heads leaned together, with the sunset behind them.

"Oh, Jesus," the man said.

"Please!" Mayumi said.

Without thinking, she fixed her eyes on the man and held up her fingers in a V, until he raised the camera and clicked.

CARDINALS

She stood naked at the open window holding a T-shirt against her chest. "Who is she?" she said, her usual half joke.

They'd been in bed but nothing was happening.

"Don't start," he said, getting up. "You know I've never loved anyone else." He joined her at the window. "I don't know what's wrong with me."

"Did you take your pill?"

Before he could answer, she said, "Oh my god, look at those birds, what are they doing? Are those cardinals? There must be hundreds."

They were lined up on their deck rails, mobs of them in the backyard trees. "Cardinals, yeah, see, the shape of the head? That sort of crest," he said.

"I thought cardinals were red."

"Maybe they're all females," he said. It seemed crazy, hundreds of them. They were all a dusty tan. He wasn't an expert, he just surfed the nature channels sometimes. "See, they've got that rosy color on the crest? The tail feathers too. I'm pretty sure they're females."

"You should have got a job as a park ranger."

It was a dig. She hadn't wanted him to take the job as a TSA screener at the airport. She was worried for his safety, even if he wasn't wanding or searching people. He'd said it was okay, he was mostly just checking luggage in back.

"Yeah, for bombs," she said.

He wasn't the only white-collar guy to get downsized in the recession. There was a lawyer who'd lost his job, an accountant, even a former pilot, all checking for bombs.

The birds seemed happy—bobbing, cocking their heads around, talking in a cacophony of slurred and sharp whistles.

"It's only the males that are bright red," he said. "Actually the females are a pretty bird if you look carefully." He was standing behind her now.

"Don't look at me," she said.

They hadn't been undressed for long. There were still bra strap indentations in her skin that stirred him. Her shoulder under his hand felt slightly damp with sweat.

"I like to look at you," he said.

"No, you don't. Are we going to keep trying? Maybe you should get dressed. We have leftovers in the fridge, but if you want to pick something up that's fine."

"Can't we just wait a few minutes? I did take my pill." He didn't want to bicker.

She sighed.

"I'll be right back," he said. He went through the connecting bathroom down the hall, to the kitchen.

The truth was, he'd only taken half the pill. It didn't seem to be working so he was going to take the other half. He'd started keeping his meds in the kitchen cabinet, and from the sink window he could see the birds, a wonderful view. The sun was just below the neighbor's hedge and the evening was luminous. At that moment the birds all rose in a burst. He couldn't tell why. They swirled around the house like smoke then ganged up in the sky over the neighbor's and were gone.

In their absence everything felt quiet, empty. Doomed, falling apart. He and his wife didn't eat together anymore. They had different TVs. He wanted to blame her impatience. He picked the other half of the pill out of the torn foil pack, swallowed it in a gulp from the tap. Even her sympathy was irritating. When he'd first ordered the pills she'd said sweetly, *It's just part of getting old.* It even bothered him that she never complained about her new job, teaching at the community college. What he was most angry about was that a man his age, in good shape, shouldn't need to take a whole pill.

When he came back to the bedroom she'd put on her T-shirt and reading glasses and was propped in bed with her iPad. She started telling him what she'd found about cardinals on the internet. She said, "I didn't think that many females would flock together like that. It says the young males look like the females, it's the older males that get bright red. Showoffs." She cocked an eyebrow at him. "They don't migrate. They congregate early in the spring, looking for food. They don't all mate for life."

"So cardinals divorce?"

She said, "Hmph," and continued scrolling, the iPad aglow on her face. He went to the window. "Hey look, they're back," he said. She was reluctant but he insisted. She got up.

The birds were massed on the deck rails again. More were dropping from the sky to join the crowd.

"They must like us," he said.

"We must have a lot of bugs in our yard."

In that moment, he wanted to tell her he loved her, but didn't. They'd worn the words out. Instead he said, "Smell that jasmine." The scent of it, inside the house, was almost as remarkable as the birds. It was a warm spring, everything in the yard was blooming, so they'd opened all the windows that morning to let the air move through the house.

"I have a confession to make," he said.

"What?" Her glance was uneasy.

"I took another half a pill," he said.

She looked at him like, *That's a confession?* "You shouldn't take too much." She held the back of her hand gently against his face. "You're already a little flushed."

"That's from the first half. It'll take a little while for the second half to kick in."

Her eyes widened and she laughed. "Then you're going to be really, really red in a minute."

He was embarrassed. Then he wanted to laugh too. They watched the birds awhile longer and he wanted to kiss her. She started to turn away but allowed him to take her glasses, and returned his kiss. A motorcycle roared down the street, the birds were still whistling, and in the kitchen the refrigerator kicked on with its usual death rattle. He wished they could be like this forever. She glanced down at him and said, "Oh."

She started taking her T-shirt off, slowly but all business. "Which way do you want me?"

BEST BOY

I was just off my valet shift, three a.m., and I'd gone to a pancake house. This was in LA, forty years ago. An old man landed in my booth, *ka-thud*.

He was one of the most famous movie actors of all time.

I didn't recognize him. I was just a kid, a year out of high school from Colby, Kansas. Later I found out his name was Boris Karloff. The original movie monster. As in *Bride of Frankenstein*, electric bolts humming and zapping, Igor the assistant, the mad doctor shouting, It's alive! There were a lot of remakes but he was the original, from the old movie days.

In the pancake house, though, he was just an old hulk in a polyester leisure suit like the ones Johnny Carson sold on TV in the seventies. They were supposed to be trendy, with these ridiculously wide lapels, but on him it was more like wrinkled pajamas. He pointed at me and said, "You were key grip. Was it for *Die, Monster, Die!*?"

People say wackos and winos are part of the fauna in LA. If they bother you, just say, "Back off." I tried but it came out like a squeak. His foot was on mine. I yanked it out from under and looked around for the cops who usually hung out there, but just then the place was empty except for the short-order cook in the window and a couple of people at the counter.

He mumbled, "No, not key grip." Then his eyes lit up. "You were best boy!"

"I'm not a boy," I said. They say you shouldn't answer a wacko, but I wanted to defy him. "I'm a girl in case you didn't notice."

"Yes," he said. "A very pretty best boy."

"You can find a boy on Santa Monica Boulevard if that's what you want."

He said, "Do they have yogurt here? Evelyn wants yogurt."

"Yogurt's not on the menu, okay? Go try a grocery store," I said. Who was Evelyn? His wife? A cat?

He said, "Precisely." Except he had a lisp so it sounded more like *prethithely.* "Evelyn's usual grocer is closed. Can you drive me to another? I'll pay you."

His voice was familiar, deep, soft, almost caressing, the most famous monster voice in the world, mimicked by comedians and schoolchildren, but he wasn't acting now, so I didn't make the connection. Apparently he thought I was a taxi, even though my company's name was stitched on my ball cap, Green Bikini Valet. Everybody knew it.

"I'm off duty," I said.

"We may have met on the set of *Bikini Beach,*" he said. A joke, sort of.

I couldn't help saying, "I know that movie. I saw it in a snowstorm at a drive-in in Colby, Kansas. Starring Frankie Avalon and Annette Funicello."

It made sense now, the terms "key grip" and "best boy." They were in the credits at the end of a movie, assistant electricians or something. I'd been in LA just long enough to think everybody was in the movies in some way, even if it was only prop rentals.

I said, "Do you know Frankie and Annette? What are they really like?"

"Colby, Kansas," he said, all evil, like he was saying, What have we here? Like he had some small creature trapped, me. "And have you come here to be in the movies?"

"I just came to find a job," I said.

"As did I," he said. "Are you in therapy? They're telling everyone now you have to be in therapy before you can act. You have to discover who you are."

He was having his fun with me, but it was okay, more kind than evil. I said, "I have a friend who's in therapy. Well, not a friend, just someone I met the other day. She said whatever you are, you have to face it. Before—"

"No!" he said, and I flinched—he had roared almost, and his eyes had grown huge, mainly because his lower lids sagged. "Whatever you do, don't face it. You must run from it. It's your only hope."

I had to laugh.

The waitress showed up. "Don't you even have menus yet?" She glanced at us both then gave me a look that said, Is this man bothering you? It was my chance to make a break, but I wanted to know about Frankie and Annette. On his behalf I asked the waitress, "Is there a grocery store around here, open late?"

"I don't know, hon," she said, irritated. "I'll get you some menus."

He reached his hand gratefully across the table, but I evaded it. He said, "We're a lot alike, you and I."

I laughed again. We were nothing alike.

But he was so serious. Suddenly he was telling me his life story. Like me, he was from a small town, his was Honor Oak,

in England. When he was a boy—a lad, he said—they thought
he was odd, thin and tall for his age with bowlegs and terribly
shy. He wanted to be anyone other than himself. So he dreamed
of being an actor on the stage. People laughed, because he had
an awful stutter. How could he be an actor? When he was old
enough he ran away. He had no skills so worked as a farmhand
in Canada and the American Midwest. He said I wouldn't believe it but he was even in Colby, Kansas, once. For years he
worked on his stutter. "It was ever so hard to overcome," he
said. In California he lucked into work as an extra in a silent
movie. From then on he was in Hollywood.

"People in small towns don't want to understand you," he
said. "They only want to categorize you." *Categorithe*, as he said
it.

It was eerie, the effect that word had on me—it seared my
heart because it was true. Everybody in Colby had me typed.
They said I was a lesbian, even though I liked boys. I liked one
boy so much I had to get an abortion. My family would've killed
me if they knew. Which was why I left Colby. There were people
I didn't want to see anymore. I didn't have any money. In short,
my life was fucked. What business was it of theirs if I liked
girls too? I got angry tears just thinking about it. I didn't feel
sorry for myself. I think pretty much everybody in the world is
misunderstood, whether you're from a small town or a big one.

It was kind of funny actually—the part about him getting rid
of his stutter, because he still had a lisp. I didn't have the heart
to ask him about it, though. I was afraid they might have done
something to him, long ago, something surgical, to correct the
stutter, that instead caused the permanent lisp. That's usually
how shit happens, isn't it?

He said, "Is that your car?" It was probably obvious—a few
ordinary cars in the lot, out the window, and one crappy beat
up little Ford Pinto, my pride and joy. A model banned from the

roads of America. "Is that the kind that goes up in flames?" He was delighted. "You're brave to drive it."

It started creeping me out, him knowing everything about me and Colby and my car.

His hand leaped onto mine. "Shall we go find yogurt?" he said. The terrible paw had me and I tried to wriggle free as if it was scalding me. "Evelyn would love to meet you," he said. For a second I went full paranoid, my thoughts racing, Is this what he tells people? Evelyn wants to meet you? To get you in the car so he can stab you to death?

His smile had grown wide. It seemed to me like death, his teeth tilted, like old gravestones. Leaving with him would be abandoning your life, I thought.

Who in their right mind would go with him?

But it passed, because I felt the tremor in his hand—he was old. Also because I defied him in my mind, *You can't hurt me*, and that eased my nerves. I saw him as just a boy, gangly and odd with bowlegs and a stutter and a stupid dream. A boy who ran halfway across the world to this pancake house, and me. I took a breath. Why not help him? Why not go with him? Who wouldn't? So I let him take me out to my firebomb, the Pinto. To get yogurt for Evelyn, or wherever we were going.

SKIN

"The man of the hour," she said. "What did you do to your-self?"

"Nicked myself shaving," Sanders said. He was lying but the Band-Aid covered it.

She kissed the good side of his face and went to wake the kids.

He drove downtown to work, the same route for more than a dozen years, including today, his fiftieth birthday, which was not a big deal. People adjust, that's what Marie said. When he turned forty she told him to quit tucking his legs up, sitting cross-legged on the couch, when they had friends over. You think it makes you look younger, she'd said, but it doesn't. Any-way it's not worth a cramp, is it? You'll get a muscle tear. She was right. It was ridiculous, vain, and now, ten years later, he hardly looked at himself in the mirror anymore.

Midmorning his secretary flipped her notepad shut and said, "Sanders, I don't believe you're fifty. Let's celebrate. Just you and me." She was his age, a mom with four kids, two in college.

They were old friends whose idea of sexy fun was to zing each other with old movie lines.

He said, "You're still beautiful, you know."

"My place. Now!" She gave him a coy look, batting her eyes.

Tyler Cullum, the kid lawyer from the third floor, rapped on the window before he strolled in. "Sanders! Just wanna say the guys and I are going to miss you at the Y."

Sanders wasn't buying. "Okay, what?" He and Tyler and two other attorneys hadn't missed their Thursday squash "tournament" in six months.

"The 'Y' stands for 'young,' Sanders. Young Men's Christian Association. You're lucky they haven't kicked you out already. But fifty? That's a red line."

Sanders gave a tight grin. "You're not so young yourself, pal. I've seen you in your office massaging that hair-grower crap on your scalp. What is it, minoxidil? Scarfing down your Balance of Nature tablets, whatever that shit is." Sanders thought of the lady in the TV commercial who said, Age is just a number and mine's unlisted, but couldn't think how to skewer Tyler with it.

Truly he was at the peak of his mental powers. Maybe even physically, in some ways. Didn't the sages say each man's true age varied? He kept thinking such thoughts all day until he shut himself up by saying yadda yadda, birthdays. Why did people have to remind you?

That night, at home, he removed the Band-Aid and examined the pink line on his cheek, which on closer look was an odd crease, maybe an inch long. Marie was already in bed. He rinsed his toothbrush and leaned close to the mirror again. His flesh was tanned, healthy, though of course with less muscle tone than when he was younger, less fat, maybe drier. Marie said men are lucky. They call male movies stars "craggy" when they get older, can you imagine a mature woman being called "craggy"? The thing in the mirror wasn't a crag. It wasn't just a faint line, it was a lesion in the skin. He made it worse by pushing at it with his fingers.

He saw no blood. Its depth wasn't really even pink, but almost the same color as his outer skin. Straddling the crevice, his fingers gently pushed a little more, and then instantly withdrew, because he sensed that the flesh underneath had moved, slithered in fact. Tingles bloomed on his back and neck.

When he stepped away from the sink, the split shrank in size to a hairline, which disappeared altogether when he turned his head. Now he caught the eye of a worried middle-aged man, ridiculous for alarming himself. At fifty his hair was dark and full. Only a light salting of gray. Most likely the line on his face was too much sun, his tan peeling in a funny way. A lot of golf lately. Clicking off the light, he headed to bed.

Before breakfast, he checked the lesion again. It was still there, if anything a little longer. Or maybe not? He shaved around it carefully. He didn't want Marie inspecting it, fussing over it as she lovingly did. If he took seaweed pills to prevent hair loss, she found it amusing. But her own crow's feet could depress her for days and it didn't help if he said, Hey, I like your crow's feet! You have good crow's feet. He didn't want her exorcising her fears by warning him about skin cancer, seborrhea, ichthyosis, whatever.

If it got worse, he could see the dermatologist in the shopping center, on the way to work. Probably it would go away.

In late afternoon Marie called the office and asked him to pick up something to drink for Joe Rodriguez and Doug and Lisa Maguire, who were coming for dinner. By evening rain puddles were reflecting the neon lights of the liquor store. At home he unloaded Scotch and red wine in the bar and put the white wine in the fridge. Marie and their daughters were busy at the kitchen counters and said hi with hardly a glance. His face was itching again so he hurried upstairs, undressed, and locked the bathroom door.

This Band-Aid stuck tenaciously. He tugged hard and as the bandage came away the skin ripped from his hairline to his jaw, the edges of the tear curling under and the skin on either side bubbling rapidly, hugely, as if air was being pumped in by a hair dryer. For a stunned moment he watched. There was no pain, only a delicate shivering. He opened his mouth, wanting to shout, which did nothing but cause the skin to detach further from the underlying flesh, leaving his face slightly raised, askew. Tilting his cheek at a different angle in the light made his skin reflect a constellation of tiny dimples, as if his facial features had been pinched into a rotten lemon whose faded peel had split.

He listened to the hiss and bump of a tap turned on and off in the kitchen below. Rain pattered loudly on the roof. Air whispered in and out of his nostrils. He felt cold and detached, like when he'd had a shot of Demerol in a hospital before surgery, years ago. The light over the sink clinical, merciless. He realized the knuckle rapping on his chest was his heart. Odd, disjointed thoughts came. If his whole outer head peeled back, what face would be underneath? Why hadn't he fainted? Was he in the early stage of shock? He thought, Call EMS, but was afraid to move, lest the skin rip more violently. Carefully, he raised his hands toward his face.

Footsteps, a hammering at the door.

"Honey, are you in there?"

He jumped. "Yeah." His voice was barely a breath.

"Honey?" She rapped again.

He shouted "Yes!" pressing his hands against his face, to hold it, and felt it slide.

"Don't be all night, okay? They'll be here early and I've still got to get ready, okay?"

The innocence in her voice, the impatience, was so foreign to what was happening in the mirror that he feared more for Marie than for himself.

He forced his voice to sound calm. "Okay." As if he were shaving. The footsteps retreated. The pressure of his palms on his face had pushed the rip wider. What was underneath wasn't blood, or bloody fat, but a seemingly normal patch of new face. It seemed important to hold the skin on, the way he might hold an almost severed finger, in hopes a surgeon could stitch it back. Yet he felt the skin insistently detaching from his face and neck. Air found its way under his scalp. He had no choice but to get it off. He felt beneath the edges of the tear and pulled. The skin stretched away from his face but stuck to his eyelids, so that for a moment in the mirror he beheld his own wet black pupil twitching at the bottom of a funnel of skin. With a shiver he pulled and the skin here too popped away. He tugged it out of his hair, off his ears, and let it fall to the back of his head. He stared at the new face.

It was almost like his old face. It wasn't as tan, but areas of pinkness seemed to glow here and there. It felt stiffer than his old face, as if some of the resilience of the old was now in the rubbery cowl at the back of his neck. The front of his neck tingled where a rip was widening between his collar bones. Now he wanted it to hurry up. With a silent shout he yanked at the loose hide of his chest, which resisted, then opened wider until it caught but V'd open wider again, as if he had popped off the two top buttons of a shirt. He struggled his arms out, inverting the skin down the forearms, peeling it off his hands and fingers like rubber gloves. Exhausted, he breathed hard. The old skin encircling his chest just under the nipples was cloudy and translucent, because of the air seeping beneath. It hung like a woman's slip or nightgown. He wondered if he was hallucinating. He thought, This is what crazy is.

Crazy or not, the skin hung there. He kept control of his breathing until his panic subsided, though not entirely. In the mirror the rims of his eyes were pink, watery, dripping, as if he were crying. The sight of them disgusted him. He thought, Get hold of yourself and repeated it.

He gathered the strength to complete the job of peeling the skin off his trunk and legs. It came off torn and tattered in places, having caught on an ankle, then at the toes, but it was almost all of one piece. On the floor it lay flat, like a pinkish garbage bag.

"Honey, are you still in there?" Marie was back, rattling the door knob. Quickly he dropped a bath towel over the skin to hide it. His own actions surprised him, as if he was out of sync with himself.

"Honey? Are you all right?"

"I'm all right."

"Haven't you even showered yet?"

"Just about to." He backed away, reached behind through the shower curtain, found metal, and twisted. Water spattered onto the tiles.

"I put your jogging suit in the closet." Her voice was fainter now. "I'll use the girls' bathroom."

He showered, carefully dabbed himself dry with a second towel, doused himself with aftershave, as if to conceal himself in the scent. He didn't want to touch the skin. He saw it had come partly unraveled from the other towel on the floor. Shuddering, he rolled it tighter, tucked it under his arm, and cracked open the bathroom door.

The bedroom was empty. Halfway into the room he heard footsteps, coming up the hall. He jumped to the bed, sat with the one towel around his waist and the rolled one tucked by his thigh as Marie came in.

"It's about time," she said. He flinched but saw she wasn't

looking at him but at herself, standing in front of the mirror by
the dresser, putting on earrings. "Do I look okay?" Downstairs
the doorbell rang. "That'll be the Maguires. Count on them being early." She hurried out with a snap of her fingers at him on
the way out. "Come on, get a move on, will you?"

He dressed in a trance, gathering himself as he gathered his
clothes, pulling on his pants, buttoning his shirt, and stepping
into his shoes. Back in front of the bathroom mirror he looked
himself over, like a stranger, and heard the doorbell ring again.
That would be Joe, solo tonight, his wife out of town. At the
top of the stairs Sanders lingered, listening to the lively warm
voices of his friends gathering downstairs. He longed to be with
them, like a child who'd been frightened. But surely they'd sense
something wrong as soon as he appeared. He retreated—what
had he left undone?—the towel on the bed. He made sure it
was rolled tight, and buried it under the clothes in the laundry
hamper.

"What are you doing up there, Sanders?" That was Joe.

He tried to reorient himself. It wasn't a hospital he needed,
unless it was a psycho ward. He had no choice but to go downstairs.

The guests were in the den, arguing about some political
scandal. He skirted around them until Joe called out, "Guilty as
hell, what do you think, Sanders?" Sanders gave a wave, turned
away to the bar and poured himself a shot. The burn almost
staggered him. He poured another. He didn't want to talk. It
was good just to hear their voices. Then the dining room lights
came on. He couldn't hide anymore.

"Come on in, everybody," Marie called, the daughters help-
ing to bring in covered dishes before they left.

He sat at his usual place.

Lisa Maguire said, "Sanders, is something the matter?"

"Me? Nothing. Tired, I guess."

Her husband, Doug, filling his plate, said, "You look pale, man." The others, Joe, Marie, all looked at him now.

He didn't want to say more. He wasn't sure he could control his voice. Crazy phrases came to mind. My skin came off, man. It's in the hamper. I had a rupture. I'm not myself. He let his voice take over, "Yeah, been feeling kind of weird. Didn't get much sleep last night."

They looked doubtful. Especially Marie. But they were busy settling at the table. They accepted his explanation. They gave advice: take the day off tomorrow, call the doc if you don't feel better, gotta get your rest, none of us are twenty anymore. Then left him alone as old friends can do, watchful, eating, resuming their earlier conversation.

He was queasy, attempting to eat. Marie didn't chide him for his lack of appetite. But his face grew warm with alcohol. So maybe he wasn't as pale. He continued with wine on top of the whiskey. Soon they were singing, "Happy birthday, dear Sanders," with merciful brevity. Later, in the den over coffee, Doug tried to draw Sanders out, telling him about a stroke of depression he'd suffered a few years ago. He'd made a quick recovery but not without a few gray hairs.

"Yeah, I remember," Sanders said, though he didn't exactly. "So did you feel like everything sort of…cracked?"

Doug didn't answer because Lisa interrupted with something and the conversation veered away. But Doug came back to him later, telling him about a guy he knew, worked for a major company, a top executive, whose world cracked apart one day in great jagged splits like earthquake fissures. The problem was his eyes. The doc told him to take a really long forced nap. That's all! So he did and when he woke up, the world was back to normal. It was stress. That's all it was.

Sanders doubted the story, but Doug was a smart guy, just trying to help, get him talking. It was nothing like what happened upstairs in the bathroom. Yet it seemed eerily on target. What *had* happened to him? Sanders couldn't say. His response to Doug was to shrug, shake his head, and smile.

Marie sat close to him, kneading the back of his neck. She said to Lisa, "This man is disgustingly healthy. When the rest of us get old he'll be the one rolling us around in our wheelchairs."

He almost felt himself again, by the time the guests finally left an hour later. He lingered in the kitchen with Marie, cleaning up, until she pushed him out. "Go up and get in bed. You must be exhausted."

Going upstairs he argued with himself, as if it were a legal matter. He hadn't wanted to be fifty, who did? He fought against it and his mind had slipped. He'd created a fault line and it snapped like a personal earthquake, that's all. A few very, very bad moments. He undressed and approached the bathroom mirror with his eyes wide open. You're not young. Don't try to fool yourself. But you're not old either. He scowled at himself a little, then relaxed his face. The scowl had pushed a vertical ridge over the bridge of his nose, which now disappeared. But lines on either side of the ridge were slower to subside. As he stared they became two deep, dark fissures in which he glimpsed the future, his hair thin and gray as dead tree branches, his bones brittle as shale, his heart beating feebly. He thought, God help me. But of course nothing would help. Nothing would stop him from weakening, hardening, and drying up.

He felt wobbly as he slipped into bed. He decided to stay awake until Marie came upstairs, to say he loved her. But the clean sheets on his new skin and the softness of the pillow cradled him, and he slept deeply.

WEATHER GIRL

They said she'd gone to Virginia to be the weather girl for a
TV station. I don't think so. I saw her tangled in the weather
balloon. I saw it swept up in the storm. There's no way she
could survive. The line was doubled around her waist, everybody screaming and scrambling. I saw the look of terror in her
eyes. Then the squall ripped her away, gusting over the campus
lagoon, shooting skyward in a lane of sun; imagine the power
of it, in barely a minute the balloon was just a bright silver
pin between massive storm clouds over the Gulf. We all saw it
on TV the next day, where it landed hundreds of miles away,
deflated and mangled across a Pensacola gas station like a giant
condom.

I'd had a feeling when she turned up in our atmospheric
sciences program a few days before that she wasn't long for us.
The way she talked about isobars and air masses, it was poetry
not data points. Me, I can read charts is about all. The night
before the storm I asked her, Why are you here? It was a big
student-faculty party and she shouted, What? She touched my

face and shouted in my ear that she'd been lonely in her room. I said, What? No, I mean, what are you doing in a little coastal Florida college program like this? She made a pouty face and said, Stanford didn't want me. We drank too much and I asked her to sleep with me.

The next morning I thought she had. Her scent was everywhere, on my T-shirt, in my head. I was late for the balloon launch, the squall was coming in, everybody was screaming, and she was dancing around trying to get untangled. She saw me running. For an instant she got this calm look of resignation that said, Goodbye, I could have loved you. Then she was gone.

The rest of the day I kept saying, We've got to find her. People were confused. They said, Everybody's accounted for, but she wasn't. In the department they said, She never enrolled.

I called Uncle Bob in Port St. Joe the next night. I said, I don't know if this is for me. What kind of college is it where a girl is lost in a storm and nobody even acknowledges it? I kept seeing her in that cut-off tee and those jeans with her knees showing. Uncle Bob had told me before I should join the Coast Guard because they always need climatologists. It was hot and I was under a campus streetlamp sweating, bugs whirling around me. I said, Jesus, sometimes I just want to sail away forever. Uncle Bob was quiet a moment. You're young, he said. I don't think he understood what I was saying. It's a good program, he said. People are always gonna need fishing forecasts.

DELBERT

It's after five. I'm into my third beer, watching the basketball playoffs. The doorbell rings. I take my time, watch the replay first. So there's nobody at the door when I get there, but I see him out in the front yard. Small, old, fat. In overalls with his cap tucked down. "My name is Delbert," he says when I get to him.

We look at the house. He's here about the paint.

"How much do you think it will run?" I ask.

He won't say. I explain how we're strapped financially. Delbert and I walk around the house, looking at the exterior trim, all he's being asked to do. His head bobs every now and then like he's listening, although he could be looking off into the sunset, I can't see his eyes under the bill of his cap.

"Has anybody else bid on the job?"

"Yes." Delbert is the third paint contractor I've contacted, but I'm not going to tell him how much the others bid. The first one was drunk and his number seemed high. The second one never showed at all.

We're standing in the driveway next to the back of the house

when the kitchen light comes on—Annie home from work—
and the light catches Delbert looking up at the drainpipes. His
face is bright, his eyes pinched to slits. Little red hawk nose, fat
jowls, two small rows of teeth.

"Can you give me an estimate?"

Delbert says nothing. Instead he's mesmerized by the drainpipes. I go up and wait with my hand on the screen door handle
until he wanders down the drive toward his pickup truck.

In the kitchen Annie tosses me the bread and cheese and ol-
ives from the refrigerator. "Turn the oven up to four hundred,"
she says. "Fix however many slices you want."

I hold the bread in my hands and watch her bending over the
crisper, picking out the good lettuce, already having changed
into her light-green ballet tights for her exercise class. I notice
that the basketball game is turned off. "Okay, so I didn't get to
the grocery store," I say.

"I didn't think you would get to the grocery store. I never
know with you, lover."

She pulls an oven pan down from the cabinet. I squeeze
her shoulders, massage the base of her neck with my thumbs
while she arranges the bread and cheese on the oven pan. From
behind I finger the top of her tights.

The doorbell rings.

"Hey. Come on." Annie pulls away, glaring.

I answer the door. It's Delbert.

He hands me a clipboard with a work order on it. At the
bottom of a column of numbers is a total: $945.

He points at a bottom line with his fat finger, white paint
under the fingernail. "Sign here."

The first contractor wanted almost two thousand dollars!
Delbert is a bargain.

It's a small house, two bedrooms, one bath. The first contractor was like one of those guys back east, a sour aftershave

and whiskey smell, the overnight kind, baggy pants like he slept in them. One of those Dacron shirts that smell like sweat even after you get them back from the cleaners.

I look Delbert over again. Stubble on his fat jowls, white stubble, white cap, white work shirt, white overalls. Clean. Honest. A pro.

I sign. He says he'll be back Monday.

Annie and I eat. I mention the painting cost and she agrees it's a good deal. Even though she works part-time days at the Del Rio Coffee Shop and I get extra for working nights at the Kruger Fabrications plant, we're both still students, and we're still stretched way too thin. But we can't put off painting anymore. The house is a lease purchase with a paint-for-down-payment, which makes it like buying a house for nothing down, then significant monthly payments. A lot of people do it. The guy we're buying from owns a lot of other houses and says he wants a pro to do the painting because too many of the people who do it themselves do a half-assed job. Okay by me. It's the kind of job you could do yourself but you end up breaking your back. Anyway, I don't want to cut into my days, which are already too busy.

Weekends are good. Annie and I don't get many weekday evenings together, so we live it up when we can. She seems especially alive this weekend, a good kind of nervous high. She's half-Japanese, a full-size girl but charming and graceful. This thing in the air between us, I don't know what it is, but I like it.

My head is still under the pillow Monday when I wake up to scraping sounds outside the house. It's early afternoon because I worked through the night, and I'm still getting dressed when Annie calls.

"That man is painting the house white," she says. "Didn't you give him the sample?"

Delbert, Delbert is here!

Annie must have driven by and seen the house on her lunch hour. "It's probably just primer or something," I say. "He's probably caulked the cracks."

"I hope it's not too late."

From the living room window I spot Delbert, slumped with his back against a tree out front, lunch pail open by his foot, thermos lying beside him on the grass, the bill of his cap tipped toward his chest.

I search for my copy of the work order, a pink sheet with some sort of heading, International Painters, something impressive like that, can't find it. I don't even remember whether Delbert is his first or last name. On the dining room table I find Annie's sample square. It's cream, almost yellow.

Outside, from the front walk, I look the house over. Yes, the eaves are turning bright white. Naturally Delbert went with the original color. The window frames are so white they reach out from the house. And Annie's cream would look murky next to the dark red brick. Not necessarily a good choice.

"Looks good, don't it?" Delbert watches me from his tree. Not asleep after all. His pickup truck is parked under the next tree down, one wheel on the curb.

I offer Delbert the sample square. "You won't have any trouble mixing that color, will you?"

Saying it that way I don't have to accuse him of making a mistake. It could be my mistake, I don't remember mentioning color before. It shouldn't cost much to overcoat with Annie's cream if he hasn't gone too far around back. "I told her she could have any color she wanted."

Delbert considers it. I wait, look down the street and over the valley, the city. A range of clouds far to the south. The west is clear, except for a blue-gray desert haze. Delbert keeps considering.

"Look, I've got to go. I'm late for a class." I don't know why I don't just tell him do it, paint it cream. I'm sure now that I did mention color. But I'm irritated more at myself than him because exterior trim is usually white. Who paints it cream?

"That's what she wants," I say, pointing at the chip pinched between his fingers.

Driving away I think, Let it be on his head. I'm not going to let this get to me.

The windows of the cafeteria at the university are open to the spring afternoon. I get coffee and try to finish my management lesson before class on whether an Erie metal fabrications plant should retool or relocate, but I can't concentrate. Let it be on his head. But it isn't, it's on mine. The guy in the electric wheelchair challenges me to a game of chess. It's a regular series we've got going and like me he's going to be the first in his family to get a college degree, only he's in his forties, ten years older than I am. There's a smile on his face. I'm going to trounce him.

He wins. His smile gets oilier after he beats me a second time. Annie will kill me. I already missed class twice last week. He's taunting me with a queen's gambit, beats me in game three. Laughs, and I have to laugh with him.

It's not Annie's fault. I talk myself into these things. By the time I get a degree so I can move up at the plant I'll need a cane and an ear trumpet. White stubble, white overalls. Hawk nose. Old but fat and strong. No eyes. I don't remember seeing Delbert's eyes.

By the time I get home it's almost time for me to go to work, late afternoon. Delbert has chosen not to go with the cream but to finish with the white. The glow extends farther around the house now, window frames, gutters, eaves. Delbert is loading up the back of the pickup while Annie waves me in frantically from the dining room window. I take my time.

Inside, she keeps her hands at her sides, rigid. She does that when she's frightened. "What's going on?" she says, looking at me and at the truck outside. "That man looked right through me."

"Take it easy. I gave him the sample. But he wants the white."

"There's something wrong with him, really wrong."

"Hey. White's going to look a lot better." It does look better. I know I'm not being unreasonable. It does look better.

"If you won't stop him I'm calling the police."

My hand flies up. "Don't be ridiculous."

"You better not hit me. Don't you hit me."

"What are you talking about?" My hand floats at the side of my vision, fingers spread. It's just a gesture I make when I can't get at what I want to say. But I feel it boiling up in me for real now and I've got to do something. I pull her hard against me. She is stiff, but she doesn't try to pull away.

"Annie. Annie."

She sobs, unstiffens, burrows her head in my shoulder. We rock with our arms around each other. It's not me she's afraid of. I will break any bastard's neck who tries to hurt her.

"Why do you have to work that stupid swing shift?" she says, into my chest.

"We've been all over that. The money. All that."

She reaches for a Kleenex, blows her nose, gets another Kleenex and blows again. She moves around the dining room table and looks at the ceiling with a wry grin. That's my Annie. Slaps both thighs at the same time. That kind of expansive gesture. It's her dance training. I don't know why, but I like to see her when she's not quite in control like this. It's a kind of electricity, a nervous excitement.

Sometimes I would do just anything for her.

"I'm going to get to the bottom of this," I say. Outside, Delbert's pickup truck is already gone.

He's done a good job. No spatters on the window panes. What I can see of the gutters in back looks good. Then I do something I've never done before. I watch through the bedroom window as Annie takes her clothes off. She's another woman, moving between the dresser and the edge of the bed, standing in front of the mirror. She is about fifteen pounds overweight but it looks good on her. It only takes her a minute to plait her long black hair before she pulls and stretches herself into the light-green tights. At the dressing table she starts doing something with her face and I think she is the most beautiful woman imaginable. My lovely Japanese princess.

But I don't go in, I'm afraid we'll argue. Instead I sit on the front porch steps, take in the view of the valley. I wonder what it is about him that frightens her. She backs her car out on her way to exercise class. Waves back at me. Everything is good now.

At work the boss shows up, a surprise visit. I can tell from his whiskey breath he's on his way home from a party. He chews me out for holing up in the office. The swing shift is over, I'm just covering for my buddy Jerry, who's late for the graveyard shift. The boss doesn't know it. He has me out fixing an old speed lathe. It's not my job and I shock the electric hell out of myself. As soon as the boss leaves I skip out to Loulou's Bar and Grill to look for Jerry. He could be in trouble and needs to know. A lot of plant workers hang out there and I run into an old girlfriend of mine who says she's meeting Jerry, but it turns out he's standing her up too. We end up getting drunk and it's four in the morning. Somehow, thinking of Annie, I manage to sober up enough to wedge myself out of the bar.

At home I shut the front door smooth as grease on grease, creep to the couch, and I'm out cold. I wake up around seven-thirty in the morning to sweaty couch pillows and profound silence. I look in the bedroom. It's like Annie was never there, though she always makes the bed first thing. Probably the sound of her leaving was what woke me. I undress, slide naked into the unmade sheets and sleep like the dead again until after three in the afternoon.

When I get up, I retch into the bathroom sink. There's a gap in my life. I think, Is this Wednesday? But, it can't be. Last night I was covering my buddy Jerry's shift, which was early Tuesday. Windows must be open, because I smell paint. In the kitchen I let my forehead press into the freezer compartment door. It's a minute before my mind can focus on what my eyes can see has happened to the dining room.

It's completely tarped over.

Empty, white. I hear breathing. The whole house smells like paint. It isn't breathing, it's the slap and drag of a paintbrush.

Delbert, in the far corner, is finishing off the dining room. The smell of paint makes my head snap. I can't get a deep breath. From the threshold I see that everything is gone from the living room too. I want to shout, Nobody is supposed to be painting the inside, but I can't. Energy drains from my arms, legs, my heart fluctuating like a bad generator. My hair crawls. He was in the house all the time I was asleep. I'm stark naked, panicky. I retreat with one hand over my crotch to the bathroom and lock the door.

I hold onto the towel rack, close my eyes. Then I run cold water in the sink, drink in big gulps until I get a crick in my neck, splash and rub my face, bury my head in a towel, sit on the toilet. Under the towel I see it. The conspiracy, how it works.

The day I call for estimates, the first contractor that shows up is Delbert's henchman. He sets a price high, way high. Then Delbert comes and undercuts it, gets the contract. The second paint contractor never showed up. God knows what happened to him. The first contractor came inside while I was watching television, he must have thought I wanted the inside painted. Was that Friday? Yes. That's why Delbert is painting the inside now. And the money: even if he is charging only $945, it's easy to see how he is doing it so cheap.

They are stealing the furniture, that's why the front rooms are empty. Maybe they put a few bulky items just inside the garage door for show, in case I ask where things are and glance in. I would never try to climb in over all that junk to find things. Meantime the good, easy-to-handle stuff goes in the back of the pickup. The henchman drives it away, comes back for more, while Delbert putters. It's an easy scam.

Knowing this makes me feel better. I know what to do now, I will call the police, like Annie wanted to do in the first place. On the phone it will be difficult to report a robbery. My picture still has gaps, there are more questions, I can't prove anything. Maybe I should call it a con game, or better, domestic trouble, which always brought the cops to the neighborhood back east, the Friday night fights we called them. I take my time in the shower, let the water pummel the back of my neck, try to see ahead: a patrol car pulled nose to nose with Delbert's pickup, the cops scrambling out and looking me up and down, Mister are you aware there's a small claims court where you can take this sort of complaint? They don't like me. But Delbert, the honest old salt-of-the-earth workman. They like him. They ask him, Is there going to be any trouble for you?

No, no trouble. I think, Get hold of yourself.

I duck across the hall, towel off, pull on my pants and buckle up, hands trembling. What frightens me is how I am ever going to explain this to Annie, I don't know what has happened to her china cabinet, the knickknacks, all that. Then it hits me: all this is Annie's doing.

Of course. It is Annie who does things on impulse. It is An-

nie who thinks that with proper management, because we have
two crummy jobs and no kids, we can afford anything. New car,
new house, new clothes, new fridge. Why shouldn't we have the
inside of the house done, now that she thinks about it? What's
one more bill? She can worry me with it later. Of course: Delbert came early this morning to finish the outside trim, Annie
talked to him before she left for work.

I am tired of taking shit from her.

I finish shaving. The house is quiet, too quiet. I peer out
the bedroom door. I don't hear anything, maybe he's gone. I
feel better. No longer naked, I am a man clothed and combed,
more confident, but still spooked, stepping through the empty
white space of the front of the house. Empty except for the
couch, under a drop cloth against the back wall. Nobody took
the couch. From the living room window I don't see Delbert's
truck. In the kitchen, nothing has changed. The little cactuses
still in the window over the sink. Across the drive the neighbor's flowering plum still there, already late afternoon sun on
the lawn. There is food in the refrigerator, although not much
because I didn't get to the grocery store the other day. I eat
some cold meatloaf with my fingers and decide to call Annie to
pick some things up.

I get her recording, *Hi, I'm away from the phone right now.* She
almost never does this. I call Mia, who works the same shift
as Annie. Mia says, "Isn't Annie off today?" There's a lot of
banging in the background and the squeal of the milk steamer.

Annie didn't say anything about a day off. It's not like her to
just walk out. I wonder if Annie is having an affair. The thought
is like I just stabbed myself with a kitchen knife.

Meantime I've forgotten to keep an eye on the hall. I defi-
nitely hear something. Almost under me in the hall door a drop
cloth flops open, a speckled work shoe kicks, Delbert rises up
in the door, his face a foot and a half from mine. His eyes

are open, wide open, gray speckled, empty. I jump out of my skin, grab his overall straps. "What the hell are you doing?" I shout, at the same time that it hits me: the consumer warnings about eating salads out of pottery bowls with hand-painted flowers or painted designs on the inside because the vinegar in the salad dressing reacts with the paint and the paint contains heavy metal, lead, deadly poison, which takes years to collect in people's testes and brains. Probably a lot of painters get it by the time they get as old as Delbert. They breathe it every day. They take heavy doses. For years it collects, nobody notices until they have crossed over the line, until they are staring up at you, empty eyed, insane. "What the hell are you doing?"

He grabs back at me and hanging onto each other we teeter into the hall. His hand flails, slaps the wall. With the other hand he's got my pec muscle pinched at the underarm, which is painful, but worse, the pain shoots to my head, like my temples are being staple gunned. I push hard and he tries to take me down with him and I give him a shot to the head. My knuckle pops against his forehead—don't know whether it's my knuckle or his skull—with an awful hollow crack. He blinks. Crouches. Twists his legs like he's going to spin but collapses against the wall. *Oof!* Pulls my shirttail out as I trip over his knees and slam into the back door.

He looks up at me desperately, eyes pinched to slits, wheezing. His cap is knocked back on his head. His hair sticks up like white straw, like stuffing. I have to get out. I tried to kill him, I think.

On the back porch steps I get my breath and peer back through the screen.

"Look, I'm sorry," I say.

It's dark inside the hallway and I can't see through the screen because of the sun cutting across the yard. But I hear him clear his throat. He clears it again.

"I need to be paid," he says.

I get in the car and tell him I'll be back with his money. Money I don't have.

I go to work early. Before I go inside I walk out on the loading dock with a Coke trying to think. It's a desperate thing I have done. Assault an old man. Worse, I can't shake the idea that Annie is cheating on me. What else could it be? Desperately I think maybe Annie went to see her sister, Gabrielle, last night. She lives a hundred miles away and sometimes Annie spends the day with her. But if it's an affair I don't know what I will do, but I will never hurt Annie. Don't be like me, my old man said.

Other things become clear. The furniture. The furniture people must have gotten it, repossessed it. They left the couch and the bedroom stuff because I was in it. And the kitchen stuff, some of it takes unbolting. Probably they will come back for it.

And Delbert. If I don't pay him and we can't pay the rent on the lease purchase, the original owner will take the house back. But Delbert has a signed contract, a lien. No one can transfer the title, the house can never be sold, not without paying Delbert off first. He has more claim on it than us.

I can't let Delbert do that. I have to get home. I call the office and tell them I can't come in to work. It's strange because I'm actually there, standing on the other side of the wall on the loading dock. It feels weird driving home in evening commuter traffic because I'm almost always going the other way.

When I reach our street it's almost deserted, the front of the house dark. Delbert's pickup is still there, under the tree with one wheel up on the curb. It looks like it hasn't been moved for days. I think about how my knuckle popped against Delbert's head, how old he is. Coming around into the drive I see red taillights. Ambulance, I think. But it's Annie's car, running, with the headlights shining into the garage. I see Delbert inside, tugging at something. Annie isn't in her car. The kitchen light is on. From outside I hear the oven door creak open. Things boil up in me. I let the screen slam behind me when I come into the house. "What's going on here?" I say.

Annie glares, looking pale, a potholder in her hand. "He was going to sleep in the garage," she says. She turns away from me and stands at the sink. "There's something wrong with his truck, he can't get home. He was folding up those drop cloths to make a pallet. Why didn't you tell me you wanted him to paint inside?"

I don't want to hear this.

"Annie. Look at me."

She about-faces, her eyes bright like she's crying, but she isn't crying. She stands with her head and back straight, lips pressed together. She has more strength in her than I could ever have.

"I thought you'd be working swing shift," she says. "There's a basketball game on, isn't there?"

I have to think. "The playoffs."

"Did you eat? I bought steaks for tomorrow. We can have them tonight."

"I'll just clean up," I say.

In the bathroom I wash my face and hands and towel off. I don't know how I could have thought she was cheating. I caught a glimpse of shopping bags when I came in. That's what she and her sister do, go shopping.

Annie has the TV on in the spare room when I come out. I see that's where most of the stuff from the front rooms is: chairs and cushions stacked and lampshades crowded under the window. Pans are clattering in the kitchen. She's left a cold beer for me on top of the TV. I sit in the easy chair. The game is in overtime, the announcers shouting over the crowd roar. A three-pointer swishes, the Lakers are ahead.

I don't know how I could have thought she was leaving. Maybe we can't change each other. I don't know what I would do if Annie changed.

The room darkens. It's Delbert. His long fat shadow, in the door beside me. His white cap pointed at the TV, a beer in his hand. In his other hand he's got a tub of guacamole from the kitchen and a bag of chips under his arm. Annie couldn't let him sleep in the garage.

I wonder if he's going to sleep in here. If he wants to paint this room too.

THE GYM

The gym is vast and almost empty, echoing with recorded piano music. A little girl with black hair, wearing a leotard so black it makes her arms and legs look shockingly bright, moves in perfect synchrony with the music. She's graceful, obviously, like a reef plant swaying in the tide. Her diagonal run across the floor ends in a series of flips impossibly, dangerously high for one so young. But she lands perfectly on the piano's last note, her arms high in a victory V. It's her salute to the judges who are not there.

Above her, three older women walking together on the elevated track have stopped to watch. The young man squatting in a corner of the exercise floor, where he can observe, must be her coach. He holds a cell phone up, as if a number is going to appear on its screen like a judge's card. But no, he laughs, he's talking to someone, and brings the phone back to his ear. He's missed her routine entirely.

The gym is now a vast cavern of silence, except for the hum of mounted wall fans. The girl, getting no response, walks to a long padded bench to join two older girls, also in black leos.

They're on cell phones, too, paying no attention to her. Maybe they never do. The smaller girl sits apart from them. Without a phone she looks around at the emptiness and gradually slumps, her arms between her knees. One of the older women watching from above murmurs, Poor thing. One of the other women says, That's life. The third sighs, Oh I know, when the music stops and there's no one there.

Below, eyes closed, the girl straightens and shakes her fingers out. Her hands begin to roll and flow in the same direction like a hula dancer's. Then her arms rise, again in a V.

ZIKA

Felicity takes the night flight from Caracas to Boston and alone in her row finds a notebook in the seat-back pocket. It must have been missed by the cleaning crew. Inside the cover, artful handwritten lettering says *Propriedad de Armando*. She touches the call button for the flight attendant to come take it. While she waits she flips through pages written in Spanish—several short to-do lists, a skimpy grocery list (asparagus, soba noodles, soy, ginger, salsa), then a surprise, a lovely sketch, with diagrammatic notes, of a striking contemporary home that seems to float among trees, defy gravity. She is reminded of Frank Lloyd Wright and wonders if this Armando is an architect. The last entry is longest, Armando begging a lover—or is it his wife?—to return to him. She sees now that the notebook is really a journal.

It's fascinating because it's so personal, but more than that, it reads like a mirror held up to her own life. She has a lost love, too, divorced for two years, every hour wanting her ex-husband, Roger, back. She's made the same skimpy, half-hearted lists, has even balled-up love notes.

Friends have been urging her to break loose and live. One insisted she accept an invitation to an international literary conference in Caracas, celebrating Venezuela's most famous poet, Ana Enriqueta Terán. The invitation had come because she has translated Terán, written about her influence on American poets including herself. The trip would be paid for by the Harvard Radcliffe Institute. How could she not go?

The drawback was Zika, a Venezuelan virus in the news. The symptoms were mild, in adults, but it caused microcephaly— abnormally small heads—in newborn babies. She does her research. Lately it's been confirmed that the disease is spread by mosquitos. One can be protected from them with the usual lotions, bug repellents. It has also long been thought to be transmitted sexually, but that's something she can avoid.

So she goes, and it is far more than she expected or hoped for. She's warmly received, and given the honor of reading her work in the famed Aula Magna auditorium at the Universidad Central de Venezuela, just as Terán herself did years ago. Many in the audience have read Felicity's book, *Abyssal Bitch, Breathing the Future.* At a party afterward, she has the most stimulating intellectual conversations she's had in years, and at a later, more intimate dinner one young man seems especially attracted to her. He's wearing open-toed sandals and a beautiful linen Havana shirt. His name is Eucario and his hair keeps falling in his face. He says his grandfather knew Ana Terán, had loved her when they were young. But alas his grandfather was only Ana's love of the week. Felicity of course knows all about this, and laughs—she likes this Eucario very much. He teaches at a university in Cartagena. At the end of the evening he asks her to spend the night with him. She's thrilled.

But something holds her back. It's Zika. Earlier a mosquito buzzed her ear in the hotel bar, in spite of her lotion, and now she obsesses on it. In the window mosquitos are swarming the restaurant veranda. Just yesterday she heard about a new World Health Organization report that Zika can hide in a young woman's body undetected only to cause microcephaly in her baby years later. She tells Eucario, "I can't tonight." She knows it makes no sense to him. She touches her hand to his cheek and says, "I can't explain."

He seems hurt, but only for a moment. Then he offers to take her to Guarenas in the morning. A day trip to visit the neighborhood where Ana Terán grew up. "Yes," she says, grateful and anxious. Yet back in her hotel room she obsesses about the mosquitos, inspecting the bath, looking everywhere, slathering repellent on her face, neck, arms, and at last collapsing into bed, pulling the sheet over her head.

The next morning, Eucario surprises her by being a no-show. Relieved, angry, humiliated, she leaves the conference early and gets the last seat on a night flight back to Boston.

The flight attendant, at last, responds to her call button and asks what she needs. "Nothing," she says. She wants to keep reading the journal now. "It was a mistake."

When the cabin lights dim she turns on her personal light and reads on. Compared to Eucario, this notebook lover, Armando, seems a fool. His words are honest, but clumsy and innocent. His lover has apparently said he thinks too much about work, too little about her. In his denial he says he loves her more than any building he could construct. She wants to tell Armando, Don't listen to her. When her husband left he said much the same of her work, long nights at her desk, dreaming more than writing. Don't give up your beautiful floating buildings, she thinks, and turns off her light. Quietly, in the darkness, she begins to cry for Armando, and for herself.

At last she goes to the lavatory, blots her eyes and nose. In the light over the mirror she looks ghastly and understands she's been lying to herself. Her husband didn't divorce her because she worked too much. It was because he wanted children and she didn't. She wasn't ready, and he was impatient. Last night she had panicked, thinking if she got Zika she would have to delay children even longer, losing Roger forever. It was crazy to reject Eucario because—besides the mosquitos—she couldn't let her husband go. Her friends would call it self-sabotage, one of the common effects of divorce, like shame and depression. Now she saw what self-sabotage meant. The knowledge was bitter yet came over her with a calm, merciful clarity, like a fever breaking.

A rapping at the lavatory door startles her and a flight attendant asks if she's all right. "Okay," she calls and flushes the toilet, a loud blast, to signal she's done. No one's there when she steps out into the aisle.

The cabin is quiet. Down the aisle she feels her life calming. She can breathe, and wants to share this with Armando. He needs to let his lover go. When she stops at her row, she has a revelation.

An airline cleaning crew would not leave a personal item like a notebook in a seat-back pocket. The journal must have been left after they cleaned. Therefore Armando is still on the airplane. There had been a long line in passenger boarding. He could have been one of the first, unknowingly taking her assigned seat, unloading personal items before realizing he was in the wrong seat. Flustered, he gathered his things but missed the journal, and moved away.

Felicity's heart is hammering. Directly across the aisle, in the same row, is a man who looks like he might keep a journal. He's absorbed, reading a thick book. Young middle-aged, wearing glasses with fashionable frames—like an architect? A man who might jot *soy, ginger, salsa* in a grocery list?

She leans toward him, holding onto the back of a seat, projecting her voice over the hum of the aircraft. "Excuse me. Are you Armando?"

He looks up. She smiles. "Armando?" He shakes his head in irritation and returns to his book.

She drops into her own seat, face hot, as if she's done something crazy. Heart still thumping, gradually she settles. Her idea is still valid. Armando could be in the row behind her, or ten rows back. She peers toward the rear of the aircraft and her heart sinks. Although the cabin has dimmed, there are still islands of light, people reading, some with faces lit by screens. But the flight attendants have begun food service, two carts blocking the aisle. Her search will have to wait.

Her energy begins to drain. She hardly slept the night before. She has no appetite. She has the notebook and Armando's name. It's a long flight. Somehow she will find him before they land in Boston. When the cart comes, she refuses dinner. All she wants to do now is sleep, or at least rest.

Soon she is dozing off, with reveries connected to memories. The intermittent soft cries of a baby somewhere in the cabin become the whine of mosquitos in her ear at the hotel bar last night. Deeper into the foggy vision, she is escaping the men. She's not searching for Armando, he's searching for her. He wants a baby but she's not ready. Just like Eucario, in his sandals, leaning close the night before, he wants a girl. And Roger, always Roger, demanding a baby from her, no matter the gender. She pleads for Ana Terán's help but can't find her.

Her sleep becomes by turns more wakeful and deeper. The baby cries again and it seems there is a swarm of mosquitos all the way to Boston. Coming up from the fog for a moment she sees something hanging over the seat back in front of her, a sweater or scarf, which becomes the wings of a huge mosquito. It's beautiful, not terrifying, its diaphanous wings folded around it like a delicate blanket. Then it fades away.

The next thing she hears is the ding tone before the captain announces, "We'll be landing in Boston in a few minutes."

Groggy, she gathers her things. Once they land she joins the other weary passengers in the aisle, eager to deplane, and only when she's about to exit remembers Armando's notebook. She's left it behind in the seat next to hers. The other passengers are pushing her out. After the briefest panic she lets go of it altogether. After all, Armando is only the words he composed on a page. In truth she knows almost nothing about him.

She comes up out of the jet bridge into a sparsely populated terminal, the other passengers streaming past her. In the dawn light reflected in closed shop windows, she remembers her vision on the airplane of the mosquito's wings, how beautiful they were. Then, waiting for her bag at the carousel, she thinks she'll never be afraid of mosquitos again. She feels afloat in a cloud of elation. She doesn't know why. It's too strong for just being glad to be back home in dreary old Boston. Then she remembers a line in one of Ana Terán's poems, about setting right "her deal struck with happiness." No one at the conference knew what it meant. Not exactly. After all, Ana was always enigmatic.

But rolling her bag through the sliding doors, out to the curb, stepping down into the road to hail a cab, fresh dawn air on her face, Felicity suddenly understands what happiness is.

She really does want a baby, after all.

It won't be Roger's. Or the baby of any of the men who have tormented her. Or of anyone else she knows now.

Her happiness will happen because it's part of her future. Hers, Felicity's.

A cab stops, the cabbie takes her bag, and asks where she's going. She stands bewildered for a moment, before she remembers her address.

At the Back Door

Longview is getting to be pretty big: next week the Good Luck Gas station will be leveled to make way for the new mall. Hoffpauer's job at the station was only temporary anyway. It's time to make his move. On this long blue summer evening he has packed everything he owns into the trunk of his old car, including the sweater knitted for him by Aunt Alice, which is too small, and the case of Wolf Brand Chili from Uncle Arvid, who owns the station. By midnight he crests the last starry hill of the county road down to the freeway and the lights of the city.

With his business degree from Longview University, Hoffpauer has no trouble getting a job in a big downtown bank, repossessing cars. They are shorthanded. Hoffpauer is tall and friendly, shakes hands with the personnel director, says hello to the vice president, goes down to the basement to meet his boss in collections, and before lunch is cruising the streets with Costa. They repossess a few cars. At nightfall they are still cruising.

"When do we go home?" Hoffpauer says.

"You gotta understand, kid. We don't have hours in this job," Costa says.

Within a couple of days Hoffpauer has it all, his own dun-colored bank car with a massive steel bumper welded to the front, his own shortwave radio, his own tow bar, his own chains.

Also, an ancient city map book. Perversely, the missing pages represent sections of the city into which half the cars he has been assigned to repossess have disappeared. He will have to find his own way.

Late into the nights Hoffpauer is still calling on his radio for directions. "This is five. Costa, are you out there?" Everybody has gone home and Hoffpauer hasn't made a single repossession. "This is fiver. Come in, anybody."

It's late, and the duplex is dark. But the TV is on. Hoffpauer raps on the flimsy screen door. A head appears, tentatively, above the shadowed couch. "Yes?"

People in Longview know Hoffpauer wouldn't step on a bug, but this is the city and Hoffpauer is a stranger, looming in the screen door. The noose of his tie is hanging loose, his shirttail has raveled beneath his suit coat. His hair is sticking straight up from riding around all day with the car window open.

"I've got to take your car," Hoffpauer says. He lets himself in. People in Longview don't need invitations, they just let themselves in.

The young man coming off the couch is small, wearing jeans and a T-shirt. "Oh Jesus!"

He begs Hoffpauer not to take the car. How can he get to work if Hoffpauer takes his car? He can't get a ride and it's too far to bus. "I'm already in trouble out there," he says. "Oh Jesus, they'll shitcan me for sure."

It makes sense. Hoffpauer figures the guy can't make payments without a job.

Moreover, "Come on *please*." He's offering cash, counted

out with trembling fingers, a hundred dollars intended for child support in five-dollar bills from a cigar box.

Hoffpauer takes the partial payment, writes out a receipt and leaves, moved with compassion, yet wanting to share his triumph. He wants to talk to somebody, anybody. He wants to call Elaine, a pretty girl with long black hair he has fallen for from Masonville, the beautiful hill country southwest of Longview. She is shapely, sweet, and skeptical, having been hit on by countless aspiring businessmen who pass through the chamber of commerce office, although her deadpan look and eye rolls don't get rid of Hoffpauer, and she can't help laughing with him. But it is after midnight, too late to crow about pestering people for payments.

In the morning, the boss is not impressed. "Shit. You're supposed to take the car." He looks out the basement window, away from the small crumple of cash on the sunlit corner of his desk. "This don't pay for your oil and gas for a day. It don't count for spit," he says, "in the bucket of what's owed on this account."

He would like to fire Hoffpauer. Why can't they, for once, send him somebody useful?

For instance, the bank wants somebody to repossess all those small planes parked in potholed airstrips up and down the Mexican side of the border, and the bank wants them now, as in yesterday.

"Boy, can you speak Spanish?"

"*Uno poco*," Hoffpauer says.

"Yeah, *uno poco*. Can you fly?"

Hoffpauer considers this. "I could learn."

The boss does a pursed thing with his lips, studying Hoffpauer. "I said something wrong, didn't I?" Hoffpauer says.

Hoffpauer is not stupid. He needs angles.

Elaine, his chamber of commerce girl, has a friend who is into debt counseling, and they tell Hoffpauer all about it. Then Hoffpauer, teamed again with Costa, tries it out on a trailer wife. They have been ranging outside the city into rural areas. The trailer wife, though suspicious, is charmed. No one in five previous repossessions, from Michigan to California, has ever offered her debt counseling before. Meanwhile, unimpeded, Costa hot-wires her car, roars and skids past her kitchen window. She screams.

Hoffpauer leaves while she's calling a factory down the road where her husband works. He gives chase in a Corvette, but Hoffpauer runs interference in the bank car until Costa gets away clean in the wife's car. Then Hoffpauer shakes the Corvette with a cutback to the Dairy Queen, which the enraged husband flies past in the wrong direction. Hoffpauer orders a cheeseburger. It's knowing the territory.

But on his own again, across the river in the now familiar territory of the city's West Side housing projects, no one Hoffpauer wants to counsel is ever home. Not afternoons, not evenings. Nobody knows where anybody is. Not even the kids he plays netless basketball with, under the streetlights, claim to know where anybody is. Hoffpauer gives up.

But comes back before dawn and gets a car. It's not where you are, it's when you are.

Most repossessions are in middle-class neighborhoods. Even well-off people choose to forget what they owe. Airline pilots, doctors, their divorced wives, young couples. Hoffpauer's friendly face is there like the diaper man, the mailman, always willing to listen, to offer them debt counseling. Sometimes they threaten to call the president of the bank and have him fired, they deride the chili stains on his shirt, they slam doors and pretend not to be home. But Hoffpauer is patient. He is always there for them. Later in their darkened homes they will go back

BARE ANA AND OTHER STORIES

to the kitchen for a beer and the refrigerator light will reveal Hoffpauer at the back door.

"I'll just be needing those keys, please."

They threaten to call the police and have him arrested for trespassing.

In the unattended hours, cars roll mysteriously out of driveways and end up at the bank. They can't find parking places for them all. Hoffpauer is learning.

Already, nobody, not even Costa, who has five kids to feed, can bring them in like Hoffpauer.

It's easy if you just keep on trying.

Elaine visits the hospital. Hoffpauer has been horribly beaten, but it's not so bad, even the best sometimes suffer setbacks, and the main thing is that the eye has been put back in. Eyes are amazingly hardy. The doctor says the cheekbone underneath looks like cracked porcelain but the outside will heal with hardly a mark. The least serious injury, a split lip, may leave a slight but noticeable scar.

"It's not disfiguring," Elaine says. "Really."

He lets her plump his pillow. She likes to look after him, tucking his shirttails in, straightening the little bank star on his lapel. He's strong and loose limbed, having been a Division III All-American swimmer in his year at Longview U, and opens doors for her. Also he says he loves her.

The boss visits at the hospital. He says Hoffpauer is the best he's got. It's not saying a lot, but it's worth a small raise.

Hoffpauer tracks a kid for weeks. The father who cosigned the note is no good, and Hoffpauer has come to admire the kid for his tenacity and wit in evading him at home, work, night school. Anyone else would have given up on him. But Hoffpauer is a professional.

At last he spots the sleek black Firebird, almost invisible under the low branches of an oak in a side yard, and discovers with some sadness that the kid doesn't even have a car alarm. It is October. Low fair-weather clouds have opened to the stars. Beyond the railroad tracks, between the rooftops and trees, are the lights and music of the Ferris wheel and the carousel at the state fair, and also in this East Side neighborhood, the muted uproar of Monday Night Football from crowded old houses converted to apartments and rented rooms. Hoffpauer feels nostalgic about the rutted yards full of trucks and cars, the sidewalks buckled with roots. The autumn air, the lighted porches, remind him of home.

Behind the tree the light in the rooftop window is on, which means the kid is in. No matter. Hoffpauer has already slipped into the Firebird and found an ignition key that works, *Vroom!* He drops into gear to go, but doesn't go. Is the emergency brake on? No. He stomps the gas and the car churns and shudders, scrabbles, screeches, thunders, billows of dust glide away in the headlights. There is the stench of gas and burning rubber. He gets out, checks around back. The car is heavily chained to the tree trunk.

He peers up at the top of the house. The light in the window has gone out. "Nothing worth doing is easy," Hoffpauer shouts.

Sundays, repossessing cars from church lots is easy pickings. On this beautiful morning while Elaine attends the Lovers Lane Methodist Church, Hoffpauer is in the parking lot of the Preston Road Baptist Church trying the ignition of a Toyota with his rich assortment of tools, thinking about his role in the scheme of things. Why are we here? Where are we going? Inside, under the white clapboard steeple, hearts are raised in song. Outside no one's around. But a stranger appears in the passenger window. His face is deadpan, sweating.

"I'll give you the car," he says.

Okay! Hoffpauer lets him slide in to scoop his stuff out of the glove compartment. Cigarettes, rags. The poor guy's hands are shaking violently. Probably a pint in there too.

Hoffpauer says, "Look, can somebody in the church there give you a lift?"

The man pulls out a gun, sticks it in Hoffpauer's face, and the world simplifies. Steeple, sunlight, everything funnels into the trembling black hole of the muzzle. Hoffpauer decides that the bank doesn't really want these cars.

Hoffpauer isn't shot. No problem. He just needs a calling. Elaine convinces him to try his talents at other jobs, and she encourages him to move in with her. He goes in for sales.

But Elaine soon tires of sales.

How often must she trudge in from work wanting a shower, through a morass of orders, invoices, commission forms in the bedroom and dining room, only to find another weirdo or loser he calls his sales force loitering in her kitchen or bathroom? Last month they sprayed miracle cleaner on her African violet, and there are so many cartons and barrels of stuff in the carport she can't pull the car in.

"What's it going to be this week? Hand goo? Neckties? Florida real estate? Just get that shit out of here," she says. "Him too," she says, pointing at a man asleep on the couch. Hoffpauer knows relations between him and Elaine have been strained.

"Let's talk," Hoffpauer says.

Her eyes are on fire. "Get. The. Fuck. Out!"

It's a time of reassessment. Perhaps he should go home to Longview.

Alone, Hoffpauer does a back dive off the Garza-Little Elm railroad trestle. Two men in a bass boat on the highway overpass side watch with open mouths. It's a stunning forty-foot drop. Hoffpauer flies backward, out over the turtled waters, falling. Whacking through the surface Hoffpauer narrowly misses, in his deep green explosion down, a submerged 1947 Ford coupe. He examines it, with its nose down and the driver's window open in the filtered light, and he is reminded that people have been trying to get rid of things since even before 1947. All of us want to get rid of things and start over sometimes, he thinks. All of us want new beginnings.

Hoffpauer is still surfacing that night at Elmer White's Barbecue with Elaine, trying to explain his vision. They have reconciled. "People have been wanting new beginnings since the Aztecs at least," he says. Rolling cloven bodies down temple steps, offering their hearts back to the gods. He remembers that from World History 101 even though he made a D in it.

"Somewhere we've gone wrong," he says.

"I know," she says. "It's my fault. I didn't mean it." She's referring to her telling him to get out. "Why are you still here?"

Hoffpauer isn't going anywhere. He takes the po'boy sandwich out of her hands. "I love you," he says.

She cries. "I know you do."

"When people have extended too far, repossession is doing them a favor." He settles her po'boy back on her plate.

She returns his smile, and sighs. "Does that mean you're going back to the bank?"

The bank wants him back. Other banks want him too. So do collection agencies, insurance companies, divorce lawyers, people who want their kids back, furniture stores who want their furniture back.

Anybody who wants anything repossessed, Hoffpauer is there.

A recession blows in like winter. For Hoffpauer business booms, enabling Elaine—who has been laid off from the chamber of commerce—to go for an MBA in marketing. The professor wonders about the big guy with the scarred face who picks her up after class, the one who won't say what he does for a living, but he seems friendly enough, and the other students like him. Sometimes they all go down to the pub together after class.

Sometimes Hoffpauer joins Elaine's church friends in their weekly poker game.

But evenings are a busy time, days too, when he's down at the municipal courthouse garage or the county records office or out at the mall, finding out what he needs to know.

Then, suddenly, Hoffpauer's there, seeking his new beginning, leaving his car parked in darkness down the street, stepping around the backs of houses and if he's not careful into the bushes and up to his ankles in flower beds. Leaving globby footprints on the little moonlit walk under the kitchen window. Up the back steps, *knock, knock, knock*. Who could it be? You open the door.

JULIE ELMORE

Tosteson erases the stromatolite cones on the blackboard, along with the circles of the Earth and the rays of the sun, represented by slashes, and the chemical symbols and whorls scrawled over everything that a moment ago he wanted with the help of the gruff excitement in his voice to resemble the Precambrian Sea.

"Arthropods," he announces.

The fan thrums. Notebook pages flap softly. It is late afternoon, not the best time for a summer course, but more than two-dozen students have shown up and stuck through the first week anyway.

"Can we do it in the lab?" asks Peavy, barefoot, first row.

Although Tosteson's usual method is to question constantly, probing, leading them to make their own wild surmises, he remains mute and motionless, staring at the blackboard.

"Sir?" Peavy asks.

Tosteson's answer booms softly back at him like the deep hammering that he and the class feel more than hear from the construction still going on in the great dome of the Foreman Hall rotunda above. "Can we do what in the lab, Mr. Peavy?"

"Make the soup, sir. The primordial soup."

"Good question!"

He continues to sweep away all now but the symbols for methane, hydrogen, water, ammonia, which he circles absently so that eraser residue grows around them like a smoke ring. He faces the class and pats his pockets.

"Sir?" Peavy asks.

With a startled squeak from his deck shoes Tosteson turns back to the blackboard and whacks it with the eraser again, as if to retrieve his thought; a puff of chalk rises and vanishes in the airstream from the fan. "The soup," he says, glaring at the class, angry not with them but his own wandering mind. He smooths the stipels of his thick salt mustache with a knuckle. Since the beginning of class he has kept stopping to pat his pockets. Why? His keys. Where are they? He fumbles among the clutter of dark shapes in the cave under the lectern. Wristwatch. Reading glasses. Calipers? "What form of energy?" he asks, keeping a tenuous hold on Peavy's question about the primordial soup. "What do you need…to generate…life…in your Precambrian Sea?"

Julie Elmore, third row, giggles.

Tosteson follows her smile with a tolerant smile of his own and looks down at his khaki work clothes. "Great Scott!" Finger marks, white ones, trammeling his thigh and chest pockets. He touches a forefinger against his forehead. "Is it in my hair?"

"Yes!"

He makes a show of looking at his palms and the ends of his fingers. They're as white as if moments ago they were burrowing in talc. "What the hell is this stuff?"

The class stirs; someone snorts.

"Find out what this stuff is, will you, Miss Elmore? Find out what chalk is made of. Let us know tomorrow at the beginning of class," he says, thinking that he can dovetail whatever she finds into a discussion of fossil seashells and the Cambrian.

"What form of energy could generate life, Mr. Edwards?"

"Electric?"

"Good, Mr. Edwards, but remember, there were no electric plugs in the Precambrian world."

"Lightning?" someone in back says.

"Lightning!" Tosteson raises both arms in a V and claps his hands. A piece of his chalk flies across the room. Heads bob up. "Lightning! It strikes the earth constantly. It's striking right now. In the mountains. On the coast. In the South China Sea. It's constant. What else? What other forms of energy?"

"Wind?" someone says.

"Yes, *mmhm*...good. What else?"

Silence, thrumming, softly flapping pages. Has he lost them? Peavy's head has lolled to one side, apparently reading a wall chart of the moon.

"Something as pervasive as the wind," he coaxes. "You saw it this morning. It's pooling around your feet right now."

Dammit, why won't they just say it? Sunlight.

"Think!" He walks out of the classroom.

They're used to him, when he needs something, going to his office, only a few doors down the hall. The keys are not in the drawer. They're not in the hidey place behind the trilobite fossil. Therefore they must be in his pickup truck, where he keeps his bourbon. That's what he really wants, a drink.

The larger problem is really the dean, who informed him this morning they're naming the new dome of the science building after him. What idiocy. To recognize his illustrious career, and all the money he brought in to help build the university. It's bullshit. Just another way of firing him. What sane man can keep teaching under a dome they've named after him? He laughs. As soon as they announce it, the Tosteson Dome, the students will call it the Testosterone Dome or the Testes Dome or the Tee Tee Dome.

Outside in the faculty lot he tries the door of his pickup truck, which is locked. He lets his frustration spike a minute before he continues on his usual route on foot, thinking of Peavy staring at the wall chart of the moon. Also the notable observation Peavy made in the first lab class of summer, while the rest of the class was describing their Bunsen burner flames in terms of heat and color. Of his own burner Peavy simply wrote, Makes no noise. It reminded him of himself when he was a gangling boy with big hands, always out of step, entranced with the world.

At the boulevard in the roar of traffic Tosteson sees the setting sun as a great orange ball of silence like Peavy's Bunsen burner flame. It's a misleading silence if one posits all life on Earth comes from the sun's heating up Peavy's primordial soup. A few easy leaps in evolution and the life the sun creates is roaring. The dinosaurs' growling is the sun's growling, the oriole's tweet is the sun's tweet, and human voices are the sun's voices, all our hellos and goodbyes, even our lies are the sun's. It makes Tosteson smile, how surprised Peavy will be to learn the sun has a voice, and it is Peavy's.

The summer's heat is fierce as he crosses the boulevard into the blessed air-conditioning of his favorite tavern, where he orders a second cold beer before he's finished the first, and realizes this is Thursday, not Friday, and that he has walked out on his class. It's like he's been gut punched. He moans and leans over the bar. It's too late to go back. What an old fool he is. The students will be gone. He understands, now, his career is over.

The second beer arrives and he's at the tavern all evening. At closing, the bar owner, an old friend, walks him back to his locked pickup truck. Another old friend in campus security lets him into Foreman Hall so he can sleep in his office.

As soon as he slumps into his chair he dreams of the desert mountains of West Texas, the first moment of his most famous discovery. An ocean of fossil sea creatures. His wife was back in camp, his daughter away in college, his students in the pick-up truck driving to the little town of Marathon on a beer run, leaving a trail of dust on the plain below. In a gold-rose light of sunset on the mountain the fossils had seemed almost alive, none of them in the literature. Countless impossible genera and species. Pteropods, crawlers, floaters. Each of which would have had its own cranky, surprising motions and brilliant colors, all of them evolving instant by instant through their own urges and choices. These simple things are monumental truths in the dream, until he opens one burning eye, awakened by voices, laughter, wafting in through his office window.

Outside it's a rowdy group of freshman students at summer orientation. Peeking through the window blinds he sees the shadows in the lot and knows it's afternoon. Afternoon! He lurches out of the chair, a sickly fire burning in his head and abdomen. He opens his office door with a bang against the file cabinet. A woman across the hall in the copy room looks up holding a sheaf of papers, the machine clunking and wheezing, her eyes frighteningly round and locked on his. One of the dean's secretaries. She waves the papers in front of her face. "Phew."

Farther down the hall, students are already waiting by the classroom door, Peavy, Edwards, others. The paleontology class.

He's panicked. "What time is it?"

"Almost three."

"What about my class? Who's going to take it?"

The machine stops, but the secretary doesn't move. "No one told me about a substitution."

Shit! It's obvious he can't teach. Not today. He shoves away from the doorframe, gives a half-hearted wave toward the students, and plunges into the men's room.

Over the urinal, he pisses a fine fire out of his gut for what seems like an hour. Easy, easy, he tells himself. At the sink he splashes his face again and again, runs dripping fingers through his hair, swishes out his mouth, pats his sopping head with paper towels. He retucks his shirt. Zips his pants. Breathes. It's not the end of the world. He will simply let the class go today.

He exits and walks with increasing steadiness down the hall. A simple speech, "Sorry, no class," that's all he need say.

As soon as he enters the classroom he knows something is wrong. It's not just his hangover, it's something worse. Talk and scuffling die down. Tension looms, a too-quiet class. Someone snickers; someone shushes. He feels awkward, can't meet their eyes. Things come quickly back: in the lectern, his wristwatch and reading glasses. Then he remembers he walked out in the middle of class yesterday. He'd abandoned the class and left them to speculate whether or not an old fool like him would ever come back.

Humiliation seizes him. He wants to sink to nothing. Then anger rises in him and his face flames. He won't be made a fool of. He can't find words. He can't even dismiss them for fear of what his anger might say. He starts for the door and almost bumps into Julie Elmore, in tennis shorts and halter top, carrying an athletic satchel with protruding racket. Late again.

"Seashells," she says brightly, sidestepping him. "Fossil seashells."

Tosteson watches her dully.

"You told me to find out what chalk is made of," she says, dumping her satchel in a front-row seat and dropping herself into the one next to it. She looks over the rest of the class, and her smile fades. She slouches.

The silence deepens, Tosteson remains rooted. He must say something.

Peavy lunges forward at the waist, as if poked in the back. He raises his pen. "We were talking about forms of energy in nature, and we said lightning."

"Peavy wants to make the organic soup," someone else says. A desk scrapes; a book drops on the floor.

For a moment, Tosteson can't distinguish his heartbeat from the distant thuds that come from the rotunda, a dull boom in his legs and feet. He clears his throat, looks over the usually sleepy heads of the class out the window to the bright afternoon, a few fair-weather cumuli, through which, at the moment, sunlight is breaking over the campus spire. He remembers Marathon, the little town near his beloved Texas mountains; he wants to go there now, this very afternoon, except for class. He can go tomorrow. He remembers he's lost something. He pats his pockets. He will find it later.

He blinks hard and clears his throat again. Yes! He remembers now. "Arthropods," he says. That's what they were talking about. He notices Julie Elmore has taken an actual seashell out of her satchel. They can talk about that as well.

"Okay to turn on the fan?" she asks. Edwards has already yanked the cord and the fan groans, notebook pages beginning their rustle.

At the blackboard he finds chalk and draws a circle. A subdued elation grows in him. "This is the Earth," he says. Because of his hangover the chalk rasps loudly as he lists the simple constituents of the planet, but he is hardly aware. He is already lost, thinking ahead. Yes—broad flat-of-the-chalk swirls. "This is the Precambrian Sea."

Then, with his chalk through it all, a slash of sunlight.

ACKNOWLEDGMENTS

I'm grateful to Regal House for awarding *Bare Ana* the 2022 W.S. Porter Prize; for Jaynie Royal's guidance in all things; for Pam Van Dyk's expert editing; and for C.B. Royal's stunning cover design.

I wrote the stories over many years in many places—Texas, North Carolina, Utah, Hawaii—with shorter stays in New York at the Yaddo retreat for artists and writers and in Massachusetts at the Fine Arts Work Center in Provincetown. I owe them all for letting me stay awhile.

Along the way the following journals published many of the stories: *Cimarron Review, Dallas Life* (via Fiction Network), *Fiction International, Fractured Lit, Greensboro Review, Hawaii Review, Hoc-Tok* (an interview including "Deep Green Lake" and "Weather Girl"), *Iron Horse Literary Review, The Journal of Compressed Creative Arts, Juked, Kenyon Review, The Literary Review, Mid-American Review, Necessary Fiction, New Flash Fiction Review, New World Writing Quarterly, Bending Genres,* and *100 Word Story.* (Some of the stories also appeared in slightly different forms in *Motel and Other Stories,* which won the Predator Press national chapbook competition.)

These works grew out of a rich environment of friends, writers, teachers, and students, and the company of countless readers who have enjoyed discovering very short stories in anthologies I co-created and co-edited: *Sudden Fiction: American Short-Short Stories, Sudden Fiction International, Sudden Fiction (Continued), Flash Fiction Forward, New Sudden Fiction, Sudden Fiction Latino,* and *Flash Fiction International.*

Finally, most important has been the love of my wife, Revé, and my daughter, Gwen. They inspired me in countless ways.